THE
SPARROWHAWK
COMPANION

edited by Edward Cline and Jena Trammell

THE
SPARROWHAWK
COMPANION

edited by Edward Cline and Jena Trammell

MACADAM CAGE

MacAdam/Cage
155 Sansome Street, Suite 155
San Francisco, CA 94104
www.MacAdamCage.com

Library of Congress Cataloging-in-Publication Data

The Sparrowhawk companion / edited by Edward Cline and Jena Trammell.

p. cm.

ISBN 978-1-59692-261-7

1. Cline, Edward. Sparrowhawk series—Handbooks, manuals, etc.

I. Cline, Edward. II. Trammell, Jena.

PS3553.L544Z459 2007

813'.54—dc22

2007035279

Paperback edition, December, 2007
ISBN 978-1-59692-262-4

Book and jacket design by Dorothy Carico Smith
Printed in the United States of America

10 9 8 7 6 5 4 3 2 1

TABLE OF CONTENTS

PREFACE

In 1993, Edward Cline moved to Yorktown, Virginia, to pursue his life's ambition of writing a novel about the origins of the American Revolution. The publication of *The Sparrowhawk Companion* is a testament to Cline's literary achievement and the success of the *Sparrowhawk* series. *Sparrowhawk Book One* was published in 2001; the final volume, *Book Six*, was published in 2006. *Sparrowhawk* has far surpassed early sales predictions to become one of its publisher's best-selling titles.

Cline receives letters from *Sparrowhawk* fans around the world and of all ages, and he frequently spends weekends signing copies of *Sparrowhawk* for visitors to Colonial Williamsburg. The idea for the *Companion* was inspired by the large number of questions Cline receives from readers who desire to know more about the historical background of *Sparrowhawk*, or the author's views on literature, or the author's writing processes. *Sparrowhawk* readers will find interest in Cline's essays on literary composition and inspiration, as well as useful reference guides to historical sources, British currency, Acts of Parliament and Royal Decrees 1650-1775, a glossary of eighteenth–century terms, and an index of formal names of characters and ships in *Sparrowhawk*.

The contributors to the *Companion* believe that *Sparrowhawk* deserves recognition for its literary quality and philosophical depth. The opening chapter is Robert Hill's "Selling *Sparrowhawk*, or Sundays with Ed," which discusses *Sparrowhawk*'s significance as a work of historical fiction. Dina Schein's "The Appeal of *Sparrowhawk Book One: Jack Frake*" explains the fascination that the novel has for readers young and old. My own essay, "*Sparrowhawk*'s Heroic Vision of Man," examines Cline's characterization of heroes Jack Frake and Hugh Kenrick. Nicholas Provenzo offers an analysis of a morally conflicted character in *Sparrowhawk* in "'He was There': The Tragedy of Roger Tallmadge."

The Sparrowhawk Companion marks the first work of literary criticism on Cline's novels. As the popularity and sales of *Sparrowhawk* continue to rise, readers can be assured that additional works of criticism and scholarship are already in the planning stages.

Jena Trammell
July 2007

SELLING *SPARROWHAWK*, OR SUNDAYS WITH ED

by Robert Hill

"I don't read *fiction*," I have heard my customers at Williamsburg Book-sellers tell me. "I only read *real* history!" Fair enough. I only read *real* history myself. But Edward Cline's *Sparrowhawk* novels, as I try to explain, abound in *real* history, telling the story of the development of the American Revolution in a way never before attempted.

The special province of the historical novelist is to make clear to the reader *why* people do what they do. The very best narrative historians cannot, for instance, convey with sufficient power and intimacy the depth of resistance to an Act of Parliament. The only way to understand such things is if they become personal. When we witness events through the eyes of characters we have come to know and whose fate is of intense interest to us, there are epiphanies, moments when we say, "Oh! *That's* why they were so angry at revenue agents!" Maxims like "no taxation without representation" just do not carry the same dramatic weight.

The challenge for a bookseller, therefore, is to suggest a work of historical fiction that will provide equal parts enlightenment and entertainment. I assure readers that Ed Cline is very serious about setting the background of his stories. Ed has an extraordinary grasp of eighteenth-century culture on both sides of the Atlantic, which allows him to move easily among the Houses of Parliament, colonial legislatures, great English manor houses, Virginia plantations, docks, taverns, and meeting places of all descriptions. He never loses sight, though, of the novelist's first imperative: *to tell a good story.* Jack Frake (introduced in *Book One*) and Hugh Kenrick (introduced in *Book Two*) are truly memorable characters. Their lives, after each finds his way to Tidewater Virginia, intertwine during the years leading up to the American Revolution, and each takes a different path toward what they know will be a thunderous clash; tragic, bloody, and necessary.

* * *

I met Edward Cline in 2002. *Sparrowhawk Book One* had appeared on the shelves of our store upon its debut in late 2001. The cover has a nice picture of ships, though one soon discovers that this is not a seafaring series. (There are enough of those.) The description on the back cover drew my attention:

> Bringing a new perspective to the events leading up to the American Revolution, *Sparrowhawk,* a series of historical novels, establishes that the Revolution occurred in two stages: the war for independence and a more subtle revolution in men's minds many years before the Declaration of Independence.
>
> Book One in this new series introduces the reader to life in eighteenth–century England, where rumblings of discontent amongst the citizens with government and Crown begin.

I thought that if Mr. Cline could tell the story of *how* and *why* this "subtle revolution" happened and just where these "rumblings of discontent" would lead, well, he would have done something no one else has. John Adams famously remarked that "the war was no part of the revolution. The revolution was in the minds and hearts of the people." But how do we in this century relate to these events? How do we bring all of the powerful emotions—the fear, anger, frustration, and of, course, the dreams, the excitement, and the most profound hope—into our own minds and hearts? How do we deepen and broaden our understanding of the revolutionary process and the men and women at the center of it?

Ed Cline's answer: write a novel. Or a six-volume epic. The form of the novel, in a sense, *exists* for this purpose.

Ed has succeeded brilliantly. His work represents a Colonial Williamsburg bookseller's delight because it illuminates as well as the written word can so many of the issues, conflicts, and changes facing late eighteenth-century Virginians and which today are brought to life again on the very same streets and in the very same buildings. Visitors to our store see a wide variety of material which can occasionally over-whelm, but few if any books offer greater insight than *Sparrowhawk* into the roots of the Revolution and the *idea* of America.

* * *

SUNDAYS WITH ED

At Williamsburg Booksellers we have sold thousands of copies of *Sparrowhawk* since its premiere in 2001. No store anywhere has sold more, and no other series of books sells nearly so well. This is a result of two factors: staff members have read and appreciate *Sparrowhawk* (they "get" it), and they sell it with enthusiasm. In fact, there are times when discussing *Sparrowhawk* with customers that we talk about Jack Frake and Hugh Kenrick (and other characters in the series) as though they are real people. This is truly extraordinary. It is a tribute to Ed's talent and his controlled use of artistic license. He has woven the lives of his fictional characters with those of historic persons, and is faithful to the record. His characters live and act among the likes of Patrick Henry, Peyton Randolph, Thomas Jefferson, and George Washington, and lock horns with Virginia's Royal Governors Fauquier, Botetourt, and Dun-more. This *makes* them real.

The other and, of course, more important factor in the success of *Sparrowhawk* at Colonial Williamsburg is the presence of the author himself to meet readers and sell and sign books. Ed has appeared at Williamsburg Booksellers many times, becoming something of a fixture on Sundays and holidays. His two-table setup always includes a highly visible and well-worn Betsy Ross flag, which helps establish his purpose and always attracts visitors. He opens dialogue with a trademark "Do you read historical fiction?" This works well because either answer, yes or no, elicits further conversation, and the more conversation, the more likely a sale will occur. Ed will also offer to the skeptic ("Are you really the author?") a photo I.D.—his picture on the book. Ed has also become adept at handling a type of reader all authors have encountered: the one who wants to instruct, nitpick, and argue. He has come to know that frequently they will buy.

Ed wants people to become *Sparrowhawk* readers for reasons beyond the obvious desire to generate bookstore sales and subsequent royalty payments. He wants readers to see what he sees and think differently about colonial resistance to the policies of the British Empire in the 1760s and 1770s. He chose to be a novelist because it is the only way to flesh out the story, to make it immediate, passionate, and personal. He can create a scene such as the following one in *Book Six*, which involves an exchange in the Virginia House of Burgesses between Edgar Cullis, a member loyal to the King and his Ministers, and Hugh Kenrick. The matter in question is a petition sent from the British ministry to the colonies in 1775: "Edgar Cullis kept his promise, and argued that Lord North's proposals were a gesture of friendship, affection, and charity, and that their rejection would amount to criminal ingratitude."

After a number of other burgesses speak their thoughts on the British proposals, Hugh Kenrick rises to respond:

> "This 'Olive Branch' is but a jester's scepter, all frills and bright ribbons and noisy bells. No man worthy of the name would accept it as a gift of friendship. Do not forget that, in olden times, the court jester alone could mock a sovereign with impunity. Are we kings who would tolerate such mockery, or men? This proposal that we bleed ourselves at Parliament's behest mocks our intelligence and seeks to suborn our quest for liberty!"

This passage perfectly distills the *Sparrowhawk* spirit. Is there an instance that such a speech was ever made? No. It is a product of the author's imagination, informed by a close examination of the historical record and fired by the need to tell a story that will have relevance and permanence.

Sundays with Ed will continue because they are profitable and enjoyable. We will set new sales records again this year and look at higher goals for the future. The market is awash with historical novels, and we at Williamsburg Booksellers are happy to promote those of merit and marketability. There is little doubt, though, that *Sparrowhawk* will retain its position as a top seller because, as we know, there is *real history* in those six volumes.

THE APPEAL OF
SPARROWHAWK BOOK ONE: JACK FRAKE

by Dina Schein

One would expect a story whose hero is a ten-year-old boy to appeal
mostly to children. One would expect a story set in a historic era to
appeal mostly to history buffs. Yet *Sparrowhawk Book One: Jack Frake*
has a large fan base of all ages—"between early middle school up to
retirement"—and of a large span of professions—"there's no real
common denominator in the professions."[1] What are the reasons for
Sparrowhawk's wide-ranging appeal?

We can find a clue to the answer by looking at how this novel dif-
fers from other stories with juvenile heroes. The action of many such
stories centers around childhood fantasies; for instance, *Peter Pan* is
about three children's magical flight from the real world into Neverland.
Their young characters typically act very much their age by engaging in
silly antics. Their concerns largely revolve around issues that are confined to a narrow age group, such as playground games with other kids,
trouble with the teacher, or fights with parents over household rules.
For these reasons, such stories typically do not hold the interest of
adults.

With this in mind, let us look at *Sparrowhawk*'s subject matter. The
action in this novel is far from fantastic or childish. Jack Frake, a boy in
eighteenth-century England, runs away from home in order to escape
being sold into slavery by his mother and her lover. Jack eventually joins

a group of men who run a business. They purchase food and other goods from those who produce them, and sell these products to merchants. The British crown imposed high taxes on all merchants' goods, which in turn caused widespread corruption, the ruining of merchants, starvation of the poor, and frequent executions by hanging for minor offenses. The men of the group that Jack joins smuggle in goods and avoid the taxes, thus making it possible for the common people to afford necessities. For this, the smugglers are branded as outlaws and relentlessly hunted to be hanged.

The life of *Sparrowhawk*'s young hero is dissimilar to the one that most children today experience. Nor does Jack behave in the way that most children do. Most children today are supported by their parents and enjoy many hours of leisure. Jack is on his own from age ten, supporting himself by working in a tavern and rooming house from dawn until night. As we follow him through that period of his life, we see that these activities, far from stealing his childhood and committing him to a backbreaking life of drudgery, make his life exciting and are a major source of his developing knowledge. Ask most children today to name what they like to do; typical answers would be things like playing video games and hanging out at the mall. Most prefer recess to class. Jack thirsts after knowledge, paying out his hard-earned shillings and pennies for an education. The responsibilities of most children today are confined to such chores as taking out the garbage and feeding the family pet. Jack participates in nighttime smuggling trips, rowing a boat through stormy sea waters, and carting boxes all night long. Between such trips he stands on guard duty. We are shown that it is Jack's unusual childhood and his exposure to the men who are his comrades in danger that serve to develop his moral character and help him mature to healthy manhood.

Jack is more mature than today's children—and quite a few adults. *Sparrowhawk* examines serious issues, such as the right to free trade and, more broadly, the proper purpose of government. It is this novel's important themes and mature characters that captivate adult readers.

Why then does *Sparrowhawk Book One* appeal to children as much as it does to adults? Issues like free trade are remote from children's

knowledge and interests. Further, the novel's action takes place centuries ago and in another country, a time and place too removed from
most of today's American children's experiences and concerns. Its hero
Jack is also substantially unlike them.

Because the novel presents its serious and complex messages in the
form of an exciting, suspenseful adventure story. A young reader can
experience the excitement of living in hiding with a group of smugglers
and evading their corrupt pursuers. He can watch Jack and one of the
smugglers, who serves as Jack's friendly much older brother, success-
fully defend themselves and a group of others at gunpoint when their
coach is stopped by armed robbers. He can accompany Jack on his first
trip to much-longed-for London. He can enjoy the respect the young
Jack gets from men substantially his senior, as they treat him like a man,
and he can see that Jack deserves it. A young reader can learn the real
meaning of brotherhood and experience the pleasure of watching
morally excellent persons. A reader, young or older, can be inspired by
the actions of true heroes and imagine that he is one of them.

Even though *Sparrowhawk*'s main character is a child, and even
though its story is set a few centuries ago, the ideas that motivate Jack
Frake and the novel are just as important for an adult and for current
times. We do not live in the eighteenth century, and most of us have
never dealt with smugglers. Yet the novel deals with such questions as:
"Should I fight for what is right in the face of opposition—or is it better
to be a docile conformist?" (The novel accepts the first of these and
rejects the second.) "Is it possible to be a heroic individual or does each
of us have inescapable pockets of corruption in his or her moral character?" (The novel accepts the former and rejects the latter.) If the
former is true, "What should I do to become an excellent person?" (The
novel shows us.) All of us—adults and children alike—confront these
questions in some way in our own lives. Their answers are of great practical concern.

The novel that tells the story of the young Jack Frake is the beginning of a larger series in which Edward Cline shows the kind of ideas
that were responsible for the American Revolution. Instead of pre-
senting us with today's uninspiring politicians, *Sparrowhawk* transports

us to a world of men like Patrick Henry—and the ideas that made him and others like him possible. It is the defense and preservation of that American character that is the true meaning of patriotism. One feels that the country whose embryonic state we are shown in *Sparrowhawk* is worth fighting for. I hope that this novel inspires many to fight for the same nation and vision.

1.   Electronic correspondence from Edward Cline, April 2007

SPARROWHAWK'S HEROIC VISION OF MAN

by Jena Trammell

Edward Cline's *Sparrowhawk* is an unprecedented literary epic dramatizing the intellectual and political origins of the United States. At the
center of the epic is the story of two heroic men, Jack Frake and Hugh
Kenrick, American colonials who recognize that any compromise with
British tyranny will destroy American liberties. *Books One* and *Two* of
Sparrowhawk tell the coming-of-age stories of Cline's youthful heroes in
eighteenth–century England. In *Book Three*, Jack and Hugh meet for
the first time as young landowners in Queen Anne County, Virginia, in
1759. As their characters evolve, their relationship deepens and sus-
tains the story's plotline and thematic development through the
remaining novels. Closely allied in spirit and in their moral convic-
tions, Jack and Hugh part ways only over the strategies necessary to
rebuff British authority and preserve American freedoms. Through
their portrayals, Cline offers readers a rare experience in modern literature: the thrilling emotional and inspirational experience of understanding historical events through the ideas and actions of morally
heroic men.

Cline has stated that one of his central purposes in creating
Sparrowhawk was to show the caliber of men who made the American
Revolution possible. Such a caliber of men has rarely been shown in
American literature. American novels have traditionally depicted anti-
heroes, alienated characters who moodily reject or are rejected by society,

characters of ill fortune and fate. In modern fiction, popular characters are often "good" detectives or spies who rescue society from inarguably evil criminals and terrorists. With rare exception have American writers dramatized the moral conflicts of distinguished men and women acting purposefully to achieve lives of intellectual and productive accomplishment. In short, the overall body of American literature does not reflect the reality of our nation's history, nor does it reflect the values of most Americans since the eighteenth century.

Why do we read literature? Because men and women naturally want to know and understand the world and to live meaningful lives. Literary art is a means of experiencing various human values, played out in the actions of characters, and the practical results of those values. Despite a dominant message in American literature that man is helplessly controlled by outside forces and circumstances, the history of the United States has abundant evidence to prove that man has free will to choose his values, to act on his values, to achieve his goals, and to find happiness in life. In dramatizing events in the pre-Revolutionary years, *Sparrowhawk* helps readers see clearly that the origin of the first moral political system based on individual rights was no chance accident, but the product of men who believed and acted upon the moral principles of freedom and of each person's right to his own life. This is the inspirational heroism that comes alive in the characters of Jack and Hugh (and other characters) in *Sparrowhawk*.

The Greek philosopher Aristotle viewed literature as more valuable than history due to literature's emphasis on universal truths, rather than just particular facts. Aristotle stated that the literary author must represent men's actions, whether real or imagined, in "accordance with the laws of possibility and probability." While history tells us what a particular person did or what happened to him, literature can explore the underlying motivations of human actions that lead to particular consequences.[1] Following the Aristotelian formula, the emotional and inspirational value of *Sparrowhawk* spring from its perfect integration of the story's intellectual themes with its dramatic, suspenseful plot. Cline's heroes are portrayed as men who honor truth and justice and select their values consciously through a careful process of reasoning. Confidence in their moral values helps them live courageously, meeting each new conflict by demonstrating loyalty to their values.

As heroes embodying tremendous rational and practical virtues, the characters of Jack and Hugh are anything but one-sided and unconvincing. Cline gives them a convincing human reality by emphasizing how they apply their values fully to their lives, while avoiding the common tendency of authors to humanize characters by inventing flaws for them. Aristotle spoke of the device of recognitions in plot development, and the first meeting between Jack and Hugh in *Book Three* includes a significant moment of the recognition of shared values. In their first conversation, Hugh tells Jack that he has read *Hyperborea*, the novel penned by Jack's friend and mentor Redmagne and copied out by Jack himself as a boy. Jack is simply astonished by the revelation. Riding home, he is touched by a new feeling:

> For a reason he could not explain to himself, he felt that some new phase of his life was about to begin. By the time he stabled his mount and stepped inside his house, he was smiling in amusement at the thought that it might have something to do with Hugh Kenrick. The younger man had impressed him; that is, surprised him with his agreement with the sentiments he had expressed in the gaming room; had pleased him with the ease with which Kenrick had made his acquaintance; had given him some strange hope of friendship. He had been dubbed a solitary man ever since he was brought to Caxton, and a near-hermit since the deaths of his wife and father-in-law. Well, he thought, solitary men are solitary only because they have not met their companions in character.

In this touch of characterization, the novel emphasizes the consciousness of the hero in regard to his values, preferring solitude to relationships devoid of common values. Later the novel revisits this theme:

> After the first breathless astonishment of discovering all that one has in common with another, comes the mutual, happy

knowledge that the commonalities overshadow the multitude of differences, and that the former render the latter irrelevant, for they have a deeper, more vigorous foundation for friendship than have happenstance, coincidence, or accident. Such a friendship becomes an inviolate continuum. When it is born, the world seems a saner, cleaner, and more welcoming place. The wearisome, aching partner of loneliness is instantly abandoned and forgotten.

Friendship is both a recognition and a choice for Jack and Hugh, whose volitional consciousness extends to every area of their lives. As the story line advances, Hugh Kenrick is portrayed as a man who genuinely prefers life in a free and more just society to his former, privileged life as an aristocrat in England. He is active in the management of his estate and active in politics, winning a seat in the Virginia House of Burgesses. Unconvinced of Jack's position on the inevitability of war between the colonies and Britain, Hugh has faith in the power of reason to alleviate and overcome hostilities with Parliament. Reason alone, he believes, will persuade the British of the morality and justice of American independence united in political alliance with England. Hugh's powerful speeches in the House of Burgesses help speed the Virginia Resolves along to passage despite heavy resistance, aiding Hugh's conviction that men who know reason will act in accordance with it. As he declares in one rousing speech, "Moral certitude is a virtue itself, and in this instance is a glorious one, because it asserts and affirms, in all those charters and resolves, our natural liberty and the blessings it bestows upon us!"

Hugh's main mistake can be interpreted as the honest error of an honest man. Hugh properly understands the motivational power of ideas in the lives of men and the critical need to defend moral principles. For example, in *Book Four*, when Reece Vishonn complains of confusion over the ideas of political philosophers and states his desire for "a politics that will spare us the tiresome, pothering complexities of philosophers," Hugh responds, "That, sir, is neither possible nor advisable. Not possible, for we are, for better or worse, heirs to their work. Not advisable, for then the encroachment of stamps and bayonets will always seem a mystery to us." While moral and political philosophy can indeed help the colonials understand the enemy's motivation and anticipate its response, Hugh's error is to believe that other men, when confronted with reason, will be honest and as willing to accept the truth as he is.

In contrast, Jack Frake is just as settled in his conviction that many men do not respond to reasoned principles but act inconsistently and often blindly according to whim, fear, or the irrational desire for advantage and power over others. Though Jack appreciates Hugh's ambition to persuade his fellow burgesses and Parliament, and later even pens an argument of his own that Sir Dogmael Jones borrows to address Parliament, Jack never relinquishes the central conviction in his mind: that reconciliation is not possible between free men and those who wish to enslave and control other men. He knows that for other men "to recognize the nature of the coming clash, to know as well as he did that there was no fundamental *rapprochement* possible between the colonies and England, these men, many of them his close friends, would need to cast off the irrelevant sentiment of filial association, if they were ever to become men of their own making...."

Jack's greatness as a character results from his commitment to rationality and his refusal to subordinate a logical appraisal of the facts to anyone's subjective desires, including his own:

> Rational persuasion, Jack sadly knew, would not this time and by itself, awaken in these men that latent capacity. Only a determined violence on their lives could ignite that crucial metamorphosis of self; only a traumatic crisis could wring from them the undiscovered honesty to recognize who they were and what was possible to them, and move them to shed the clinging, comfortable traces of their past lives. Only the glint of approaching bayonets, or the thunder of a volley, or the calculated toss of a torch into their homes would give them long enough pause to allow the truth about themselves and what they were witnessing to seize their beings and awaken in them the true nature of their peril. If Hugh Kenrick, the proudest, most honest, most vir-

tuous, most complete, and most thoroughly rational man he had ever known, could not be persuaded of the logic of events, then how could he expect other men…to be persuaded so soon of that logic?

In *Sparrowhawk*, the central conflict is seen, not in the struggle between the colonies and England, but in the relationship between Jack and Hugh, two virtuous men pursuing rational values. Though on different roads to their destination, Jack and Hugh recognize the same spirit and soul in one another. For Jack, Hugh is "a self that would never submit to malign authority; a self that was sensitive to the machinations of others, a self trained in the brittle, lacerating society of the aristocracy to be on guard against sly encroachments; a self that was proof against corruption, sloth, and violence; a self that recognized and cherished itself, and so was proud; a self that quietly gloried in its own unobstructed and unconquered existence. A self very much like his own."

In *Sparrowhawk*, Cline portrays his heroes with a consistent emphasis on values in action. Each plot event is related to the characters' moral values, and the plot is tightly structured upon the characters' pursuit of their values. Absent in *Sparrowhawk* are pointless plot digressions unrelated to the story's major themes or "humanizing" touches of characterization that detract from the heroes' moral stature. As fictional characters, Jack and Hugh achieve a compelling reality through Cline's focus on the chosen moral values that shape his characters' minds and motivate their actions. The portrayal of free will, rationality, moral grandeur, and the integrity of the heroes' souls convince readers that Jack and Hugh indeed represent what is possible to all men.

1.   See Chapter 9, Aristotle, *On the Art of Poetry* (*Classical Literary Criticism*, London: Penguin, 1965).

"HE WAS THERE":
THE TRAGEDY OF ROGER TALLMADGE

by Nicholas Provenzo

The value of tragedy in romantic literature rests in its ability to illustrate a warning: *Do not choose this—avoid this path*. In *Sparrowhawk Book Six: War*, novelist Edward Cline presents his readers with the tragic death of British Army Captain Roger Tallmadge during the battle of Bunker Hill. Tallmadge's death at the hands of *Sparrowhawk* hero Jack Frake is lamentable in that Cline presents Tallmadge as an upright and moral man, yet a man without sufficient vision to boldly and consistently break free of the chains of tyranny that shackle him, as well as the American colonists. Cline presents Tallmadge as dying in the very service of the forces that ensnare him.

To fully appreciate the intricacies of Tallmadge's tragedy, we must first establish who he is in relationship to *Sparrowhawk*'s main characters. The neighbor of Hugh Kenrick's family in England, Tallmadge is married to Hugh's sister Alice, and he thinks of Hugh as an elder brother and moral exemplar. To Hugh, Tallmadge represents Kenrick's affinity for his home country—an affinity strained by the crown's ruthless mistreatment of the American colonists and of Hugh's martyred Pippins—yet an affinity that exists nevertheless. In fact, Tallmadge's virtue and sympathy for the plight of the American colonists helps buoy Hugh's hopes for a possible reconciliation between the colonists and a more civil England.

Tallmadge serves as an artillery officer in the British Army, seeing both combat and attaché duty in Europe, and he faithfully discharges his responsibilities. He is entrusted with the important mission of reconnoitering the American colonies and reporting the state of the colonists' political sentiments and military readiness to his commander General Gage. When visiting Hugh's plantation in Virginia, Tallmadge joins him in drawing swords and preventing the looting of Jack Frake's Morland Hall by arch villain Jared Hunt and his gang of customs men and Royal Marines.

In such instances, Cline presents Tallmadge as acting valiantly in defense of the good, yet in a political and moral universe such as Tallmadge's, his good deeds cannot go unpunished. He is betrayed by his jealous and scheming subordinate, along with Jared Hunt and his allies, and his treason in Virginia is revealed to General Gage. Hoping to leave military service and return to England and a seat in Parliament, Tallmadge is instead ordered by a magnanimous General Gage to remain in the colonies for another year rather than face the disgrace of certain court-martial in England.

It is at this time that Tallmadge places his tin gorget, a gift from Hugh inscribed with the words "A Paladin for Liberty," at the bottom of his baggage, a poignant metaphor for his future actions. Tallmadge prepares his men for the inevitable clash with the American colonists and witnesses the British retreat from Lexington and Concord. Tallmadge writes to Hugh of his experiences, and these letters serve to contrast Tallmadge's own mixed feelings over the injustice of the brewing conflict with his recognition of the grimly determined colonial spirit, as portrayed through his haunting, yet admiring account of a mortally wounded colonial militiaman spitting his last breath in contempt against his would-be overlords at Lexington Green.

Clearly Tallmadge does not want to engage the colonists in battle. He again expresses to Hugh in his letter that he wishes he would be relieved of his command and allowed to return to England, where he believes he can press for the colonial cause in Parliament. And thus it is here where Tallmadge's choices turn tragic. The time for speaking has long ended; there is no one in power in England willing to even listen to the colonists' grievances, let alone willing to work to correct them. The machinations of ruthless men have deprived the colonists of their wealth, their freedom, and even the vague pretense that they enjoy the rights of Englishmen.

Worse for Tallmadge, it is precisely his virtues that are exploited for the purpose of subjugating the colonists. His efficacy as a commander, the loyalty he earns from his men, his level head and gallantry under fire are all used in furtherance of a purpose that he does not support. His life is placed in peril, yet he refuses to resign his commission or even acknowledge the possibility of such a choice. It is this failure to act that ultimately costs Tallmadge his life.

As Tallmadge and the redcoats stand upon one end of the battlefield of Bunker Hill, Jack Frake and his company of independent Virginia militiamen stand upon the other. In the contest between these two forces, Frake fires his musket at Tallmadge (whom he does not recognize until after his shot has been fired), striking dead this man who had once saved his home, dined at his table, and had been described as a man of honor by none other than Frake himself. Frake is not a man who sought to kill any Briton, but as one who realizes that their choices made it necessary. Frake's internal questioning of his actions are short-lived, for he recognizes that Tallmadge willingly allowed himself to be placed between the colonists and their right to their lives, and that such a choice could be paid for only with Tallmadge's own life.

Thus the tragedy of Roger Tallmadge reveals itself to be the tragedy of the half-fought battle—an internal conflict within a man who acts boldly when evil exists clearly before his eyes, yet who is unable to apply the same principles that initially compelled him to act upon broader and more abstract conflicts. Why would Tallmadge risk himself and his career in order to save Jack Frake's home, only to dutifully serve with the forces that fought to attack all of the colonists' homes—and threaten the colonists' very lives? What mental error permits a man to willingly sacrifice himself in such a grotesque manner? As Frake coldly observes when he reports Tallmadge's death to a distraught Hugh Kenrick, "[Tallmadge] couldn't both sympathize with [the colonists'] cause, and help to crush it, too."

Jack states a fact about Tallmadge which Hugh cannot ignore: "He was there."

At root, Tallmadge's error lay with his failure to grasp the true meaning of the American Revolution and apply its maxims to his own life. As Cline notes through the wisdom of his hero Hugh Kenrick, "One owns one's own life; it is a thing that was never theirs to grant or give, covet, own, or expend; it is a thing never to be granted or surrendered to others, regardless of their number or purpose." And as Cline, through Hugh Kenrick observes, "That truth is the source of all the great things possible in life." Had Tallmadge taken full ownership of his own life, he would not have allowed its course to be piloted by those whose values and aims he did not share. Even if he would have still met death in the process, he would met death as a free and independent man, and not the mere pawn of others. For all his intelligence, virtue, and courage, Tallmadge ultimately stood disarmed against his real opponents. For this, he only had himself to blame.

It may be tempting for some today to look upon the tragedy of Roger Tallmadge with the knowledge of the colonists' ultimate victory and blithely claim that they would never make such an error; that each of us would choose to act consistently in support of their freedom. It is the sad tenor of our times though that men and women bestowed with the birthright of freedom nevertheless willingly sacrifice their freedom, property, and very lives to lesser opponents than the founding patriots knew when facing down the power of the British Empire.

And thus the same question John Proudlocks asks a mournful Hugh Kenrick can just as easily be asked of us: "Between Jack and Captain Tallmadge, which man would you choose as a greater sibling in spirit to you?"

THE WAYS, MEANS, AND ENDS
OF *SPARROWHAWK*

by Edward Cline

This essay is included with the confidence that it will not spoil a reader's enjoyment of the *Sparrowhawk* novels if he has not yet read any of them; there are a number of "plot spoilers" in it, none of them key. Those who have read the series, however, have often wondered how and why I undertook the writing of this epic. I have never been reluctant to discuss those matters and welcomed the opportunity to put my answers on record.

Other readers, sensing the difference between *Sparrowhawk* and most contemporary literature and other American historical novels set in this period, have expressed surprised and pleased astonishment that it ever saw the light of day, but could not express the difference. That is one of the tasks of this essay, to identify the difference. I will say here that I had not expected *Sparrowhawk* to see daylight, at least not in my lifetime. Fortunately, against all the odds and against all the advice and wisdom of undertaking such a project, the series found a champion in its publisher, David Poindexter, founder of MacAdam/Cage and a restless rebel in his own right. The story goes that after he had finished reading the manuscript of *Book One: Jack Frake*, and knowing that I was at work on *Book Four: Empire*, and that I had two more titles in the series to complete, he wrote on top of his reader's report: PUBLISH.

* * *

SOME HELPFUL LITERARY DISTINCTIONS

Where does *Sparrowhawk* fall in the literary scheme of things? Is it a Romantic novel? A historical novel? Or perhaps a combination of both genres? Let me briefly examine these questions.

"Romanticism is a category of art based on the recognition of the principle that man possesses the faculty of volition," wrote Ayn Rand in 1969.[1] In 1968, she wrote, "Romanticism is the *conceptual* school of art. It deals, not with the random trivia of the day, but with timeless, fundamental, universal problems and *values* of human existence. It does not record or photograph; it creates and projects."[2]

In *Ayn Rand Answers*, she explains the difference between Romanticism and Romantic Realism. "My school of writing is romantic realism: 'romantic' in that I present man as he ought to be; 'realistic' in that I place men here and now on this earth, in terms applicable to every rational reader who shares these values and wants to apply them to himself. It is realistic in that it projects man and values as they ought to be, not as statistical averages."[3]

Again, in "What is Romanticism?" Rand dwells on the necessity of volition and moral values in Romantic fiction: "The events in their plots are shaped, determined and motivated by the characters' values (or treason to values), by their struggle in pursuit of spiritual goals, and by profound conflicts."[4]

In that sense, *Sparrowhawk* is not "realistic." Its time frame is not "here and now," but centuries ago, before our time, although the rational values its characters hold and fight for are indubitably applicable to any reader with a measure of self-esteem living today. *Sparrowhawk* is an epic and, from particular perspectives, also an allegory on our own times, a celebratory reminder of our glorious past, and a reprimand to those who would prefer that we forget it.

* * *

ON THE ROLE OF FICTION
IN FICTION

Among the various themes present in the series, *Sparrowhawk* is also about *Hyperborea*, that is, about the crucial role of art in one's life. The fictive novel, whose full title is *Hyperborea: or, the Adventures of Drury Trantham, Shipwrecked Merchant in the Unexplored Northern Regions*, gives Jack and Hugh an idea or vision of a moral ideal in the character of Drury Trantham. Although they move themselves, and become sculptors of their own souls, *Hyperborea* both affirms their vision of life and accelerates their development as heroes in their own right. The details of that novel I intentionally left sketchy; they were not important. What was important was what Jack and Hugh did about living up to the spirit of the novel. Jack and Hugh are already moral men when they first encounter *Hyperborea*—Jack, when he is a member of a band of smugglers who defy the Crown on principle; Hugh, as a member of the aristocracy when he violates one of its most oppressive customs and cannot concede the transgression.

Drury Trantham, the hero of *Hyperborea*, sailing on his renegade ship, the *Greyhound*, is Redmagne's romanticized projection of his own life as an outlaw. Trantham discovers a "utopia" that is limited only by Redmagne's imagination. Where is Hyperborea? According to the *Smaller Classical Dictionary*, it was a land of "perpetual sunshine, beyond the north wind." Hyperborea's name is comprised of the Greek *huper*, or extreme, and *boreios*, or northern.

"It's a wonderful story," Redmagne tells Jack one evening, "about a land much like our own, but where there are no kings, no customs men, and no caves...No kings! Can you imagine it? No kings, and so no need for all the varieties of Danegeld! It's an allegory, you see, because Hyperborea was once in thrall to another kingdom, the kingdom of Hypocrisia. But Hyperborea threw off its bondage, and became a happy land, a great land, a prosperous land. Suppose—Oh! Wild imagination!—suppose our colonies in America did such a thing?...What an outlandish miracle that would be! Perhaps too far-fetched!"[5]

He goes on to tell Jack, whom he will draft in the task of copying out the manuscript of his completed novel, that the Hyperboreans are a "race guided by nothing but reason...Drury Trantham elects to stay with them...because he finds nothing impossible and everything wonderful about them. They live on an island in the frigid climes, but their greatness warms the earth and makes it habitable."

But, *what* is Hyperborea? It is America, an idea and a place they—Redmagne, Skelly, Glorious Swain, Jack Frake, and others in the story—can only imagine and project from the uncorrupted, unvanquished cores of their souls. The spirit of what they think is possible is best captured in a memorable line uttered by Greta Garbo in *Queen Christina*: "One can feel nostalgia for places one has never seen." Jack Frake and Hugh Kenrick, however, while they initially can only imagine the possible, later help to create it and live to see it.

I invented a novel that both Jack Frake and Hugh Kenrick could be moved by. That was *Hyperborea*. No other actual novel of the period did that job. It is a kind of *The Fountainhead* for them, a work of art that said "Yes" to their characters and values. And *Hyperborea*'s own story had to be thematically integrated in the story. An outlaw writes it, and an aristocrat envisions its possibilities. And both Jack and Hugh eventually come to Hyperborea, or America, and emulate some of the principal events in the novel. At the same time, the novel had to be of the period, with a story that anticipates the Romantic novel of the nineteenth century. Neither Jack nor Hugh could find inspiration in any of the Naturalist novels of the period, such as *Tom Jones* or *The Vicar of Wakefield*.

The novel and its hero serve to unify Jack's and Hugh's relationships between them and with other characters. Jack idolizes Redmagne and Skelly, for they are both moral men of action who become outlaws because they will not submit to fiat authority. Hugh admires the daring freethinkers of the Society of the Pippin; their wide-ranging intellectual curiosity and vitality match his own. It is an important plot development that Jack and Hugh encounter the novel after they have made crucial decisions in their lives: Jack, after he has joined the smuggling gang and grasps the reason why its members choose to be outlaws; Hugh, after he refuses to apologize for neglecting to bow to the Duke of Cumberland. Redmagne's novel affirms the importance of those decisions.

How can the heroes in such fiction have the attribute of volition when the important events in such fiction are a matter of record? How could they contribute to such events? Should historical events or a particular period serve as a background to one's story, or be integrated into the conflict of one's characters? Is it proper to portray historical figures in those events (such as Jefferson or Washington); that is, to put words into their mouths and actions in their careers, and if so, how should they be characterized or *not* characterized?

The answer to the first two questions is: *Integration* of plot and character. Someday I will pen my own essay on the subject of historical fiction. For the time being, I would refer anyone to Rand's *The Art of Fiction*, and *The Romantic Manifesto*, in addition to *Essays on Ayn Rand's "Anthem"* and *Essays on Ayn Rand's "We the Living."*

The liberties with which some novelists and film directors have taken with the portrayals of historic personages have intrigued, troubled, or baffled me. The portrayals largely have been bizarrely gratuitous, or forgettably superficial, or memorably malicious. Rarely have such portrayals been accurate. Two instances in film come to mind: *Amadeus* and Peter Shaffer's unwarranted "feet of clay" characterizations of Mozart and Antonio Salieri, and the portrayal of genius as inexplicably subjective and irrational; versus *Khartoum*, in which the portrayal of General Charles Gordon as a religiously motivated man in conflict with the Mahdi, a Muslim jihadist of the nineteenth century, was proper and credible.

I think there is a single rule that would govern the proper portrayal of a historic personage in fiction: that it should not contradict or exaggerate the known about that personage, whether the known is good or bad, especially if a writer can grasp, delineate, and dramatize a personage's fundamental character. Thus, in *Sparrowhawk*, George Grenville, author of the Stamp Act in 1765, by all written accounts of his words and actions, can be portrayed as a scheming manipulator who overstepped his brief stay as prime minister in his quest for power and fame. William Pitt can be portrayed as a moody, enigmatic vessel of tragic contradictions. Patrick Henry can be portrayed as a passionate advocate of liberty. And Thomas Jefferson's portrayal from *Book Three: Caxton* to the end of the series can chart his progress and maturation from a law student contemplating a stable career as an attorney to an intellectually and politically active patriot.

* * *

A LITERARY AMBITION

Although the American Revolution has been the subject of fiction, it is the war of 1776–1781 that has been the focus of most novelists. The period preceding the war has been largely neglected in terms of dramatizing its fundamental character. It is that period I chose as a setting for the conflicts in *Sparrowhawk*. One important attribute of a credible dramatization of the causes of the American Revolution is the creation of the characters of the men who made it possible, of the intellectual and moral caliber of such men who subscribed to those ideas and acted on them. The men must match the ideas. Crucial to that task was creating characters who were distinct individuals, and not mere hollow vehicles of the ideas that moved men in that time.

I began researching the pre-Revolutionary period in late 1992, when I was living and working in Palo Alto, California. By then *First Prize* and *Whisper the Guns* had been published (1988 and 1992 respectively). And by then I had written nine novels—detective and suspense novels in three separate series—only two titles of which had been published, and a miscellany of nonfiction—book reviews, guest editorials, and the like.

However, I had always wanted to write something about the Revolution, but did not want to settle for the standard costume drama. My detective and suspense novels were, in a sense, mere training to write this series. Nor was I satisfied that novels such as Cooper's *The Last of the Mohicans* set in the pre-Revolutionary period did justice to the period (not that Cooper and other novelists intended that; they were merely writing adventure stories). It was my conviction that a great vacuum existed in American literature that dealt with the founding of the United States. Britain, France, Spain, and other countries had their "national" literatures. But the United States did not.

Nor was I content with the comparatively fewer novels that were set in the period, such as *Citizen Tom Paine* and *Oliver Wiswell*, and which were written by leftists or writers demonstrably ignorant of the period. They were what I would call "surfacy"; that is, superficial and not credible. Most of them treated such concepts as "liberty" and "freedom" as floating abstractions. What I wanted to do was write a novel that dealt with the ideas that moved the men of that period, and to dramatize the moral and intellectual caliber of the men who were passionately moved by those ideas.

One thing that convinced me I was ready in 1992 was the most recent remake of James Fenimore Cooper's *The Last of the Mohicans*. I was appalled by not only how the director turned Cooper's story around, but by how little time, about five seconds, was devoted to the conflict between Britain's imperial interests and the colonials. There is much more of that in the novel.

Did I know I was writing an epic? In the beginning, not quite. But by the time I was finished with *Jack Frake*, I knew it was going to be an epic—had to be an epic. And when I surveyed American literature, I saw that there was nothing (except for Ayn Rand's novels) in it that attempted to capture the American character and perspective on life in their most fundamental terms, nothing that portrayed men as distinct individuals governed by reason. It was a glory that had rarely been recognized, rarely addressed in fiction.

I had originally conceived of the project as a two-volume novel. But as I finished *Book One: Jack Frake*, I saw that it was going to be much, much longer, if I were going to properly handle all the themes and subplots and reach the end and resolutions I had already worked out. And by that time I was completely immersed in the period—grasping the politics, the culture, the standard of living, the manners, customs, and traditions—and mastering all the elements to recreate the British-American culture and politics that existed then.

Also, at that time, I hadn't the least hope that the novels would ever find a publisher and see the light of day. Publishing standards were declining, and so was literacy. I had difficulty finding an agent to represent my relatively inoffensive detective and suspense novels, never mind a multivolume historical novel. But, I didn't care. This story had to be told, the novel written, completed, and made real, regardless of personal cost. It was an exercise in preserving my own sanity, to bring the story into existence.

One task I mastered was writing in spoken and written eighteenth-century British English, on different levels. Then I learned how to scale that language back for modern readers. In a novel of ideas, dialogue is more important than physical action and is actually action of a sort; it makes important physical action possible and far more effective and memorable. I love writing dialogue; it can be just as telling as action.

Music plays an important role in the series. Music, especially nineteenth-century and early twentieth-century classical music, has always fed my imagination, as do, to a lesser extent, film scores composed according to the rules of classical composition.

It is probably a universal truism that what others hear in classical music is not what inspired its composers, and my response to a particular symphony or concerto would not necessarily have much in common with what it evokes emotionally in someone else. My favorite pieces are scores to stories of my own invention. The classical music of the eighteenth century little appealed to me before I began researching *Sparrowhawk*. But as I listened to more of it, in search of music that might move Jack and Hugh, and also to grasp the character of the best music of the period, I acquired a taste and found roles for much of what the period had to offer, including many "folk" melodies, some of which, such as "Hugh O'Donnell" and "Brian Boru," Etáin plays on her harp during a Caxton concert.

The three composers who offered the most material for the story were Georg F. Handel, Alessandro Scarlatti, and Antonio Vivaldi. Two compositions by Handel and Scarlatti became personal "anthems" of Jack and Hugh, and both are played by Etáin: "See, the conquering hero comes" from Handel's *Judas Maccabæus*, and the Recitativo and Andante from Scarlatti's "Cantata pastorale per la nativitá di nostro signore Gesu Cristo" ("A pastoral cantata on the nativity of Jesus Christ").

These selections have nothing to do with their religious origins; the elevated spirits they celebrate evoke the core souls of Jack Frake and Hugh Kenrick. Vivaldi's "Echo Concerto for Two Violins" (RV535) and his Cello Concerto (RV413) also provided thematic substance.

When I began work on *Book Three: Caxton*, I found I was losing track of my secondary characters. I began a list that now numbers over 370 names of characters that identifies who they are and where in the series they appear. The project also entailed creating a subject index for all the information amassed from my research in eight notebooks, in addition to a glossary of eighteenth-century terms.

Most of my "fans" are delighted, if not ecstatic, that the series exists not only to enjoy, but because it can also be used as a virtual history text. I can only describe the common response to it as "jaw-dropping." Many people who come to my booksigning table will read a few paragraphs from one of the titles, then make up their minds on the spot that they must have that title or all of them. Many Americans had simply given up on American fiction, especially fiction that celebrated this country's founding and did not attempt to dilute its significance with the poisons of "diversity" and "multiculturalism."

I am especially happy that young readers become engrossed with the novels. It is a phenomenon that apparently is occurring around the country. I suppose one could argue that I am a member of the intelligentsia, and that I am helping to point Americans in the right direction, in terms of philosophy, politics, moral values, and aesthetic values. I tell people at booksignings that the reading age range of the series, from what I've observed in three years of signings, is between 10 years and retired. I was certain there was a potential readership, but proof of its existence has surpassed my wildest expectations.

* * *

THE DEDICATIONS

A word or two about the dedications. The first, which occurs in the beginning of *Books One* through *Three*, is adapted from the 79th edition of *Pears Cyclopædia* (1970). The full quotation, under the section "The Contemporary Theatre," following the heading, "The Function of Dramatic Art," is: "The especial province of drama, as was pointed out by Aristotle, is to create an image, an illusion of action, that action 'which springs from the past, but is directed towards the future, and is always great with things to come.' Both tragedy and comedy depict such action and the conflict which it normally entails."[6]

While the quotation captures the essence of Aristotle's philosophy of drama, the fragment within the above quotation, ostensively ascribed to Aristotle, is not to be found in the *Poetics* or in any other book of his works. The entire paragraph in which it occurs doubtless was written by someone who understood Aristotle.

However, a query to the *Pears* editors was answered with the unfortunate news that, after a passage of thirty years, not only had all the back matter and manuscripts for that edition of the *Cyclopædia* been discarded, but the staff and contributors to it had since passed on. Aristotelian scholars could find nothing resembling the fragmentary quotation, though they could not contest its meaning. This particular dedication was meant to underscore the moral development of Jack Frake and Hugh Kenrick, together with heralding the story and the sequence of events beginning with the first page of *Book One*.

The second dedication—"To hold an unchanging youth is to reach, at the end, the vision with which one started"—which occurs in *Books Four* through *Six*, is taken from Ayn Rand's novel, *Atlas Shrugged*, and is almost self-explanatory. It, too, underscores the vision that moves Jack Frake and Hugh Kenrick, and is a suggestion to readers that they rediscover the vision that moved the Founders to create this country. The Founders and my characters take the received wisdom of the Enlightenment to its limits, but no further. It remained for Rand to pick up from Aristotle's and the Founders' legacies, fill in most of the blanks that they left behind, then revise the whole page.

The Founders cannot be faulted for not having gone beyond their received wisdom. They were extraordinary moral and political practitioners, not philosophers. There was no Ayn Rand to point out their errors and purge their political philosophy of its flaws. It must be noted that when the Founders were active and reaping the benefits of the Enlightenment and applying its ideas to politics, philosophers such as Immanuel Kant and David Hume in that period were active in sabotaging the Enlightenment, just as their heirs today, who promulgate a repellant, destructive mix of pragmatism, nihilism, and subjectivism, are gnawing at the remnants of Western civilization. In the Founders' time, John Locke was the high point of political philosophy, and it was on his work that they based their moral arguments and justified their actions.

One cannot gainsay the Founders, as their many contemporary detractors try to today. They never professed to be infallible. Consider what they accomplished, the freest country in history, and the first one in history founded on a set of ideas, a political entity, whatever its shortcomings and flaws, that addressed and complemented the nature of man who requires reason and the freedom to exercise it to survive and prosper.

* * *

FACT VS. FICTION

An absence of evidentiary proof for a novelist, especially one who writes historical fiction, is a natural invitation to employ "artistic license." In the course of researching and writing the *Sparrowhawk* series, I encountered numerous such opportunities. On one hand, there was an overabundance of historical data that enabled me to fashion a credible recreation of events in the eighteenth century conflict between Britain and her American colonies, events that would be the focus of the drama in the story, or events as background to the story.

On the other hand, key events, such as the debates and adoption of Patrick Henry's Stamp Act Virginia Resolves in May 1765, were not so well documented. They were enveloped in a haze of approximation, educated speculation, and scholarly guesswork. Little or nothing could be factually established. For example, only fragments of Henry's defiant speech survive—such as, "If this be treason, then make the most of it"—

and are the recollections years after the event of men who heard him that glorious day.

As a rule, colonial orators rarely recorded their own speeches, and if we have renditions of them, it is thanks to those so moved by them that they sat down and wrote them out. The journals of the House of Burgesses dryly record only votes and subjects discussed and actions taken, but no speeches by any member of that body. So, lost to us are not only Henry's words, but those of his allies and enemies in that chamber.

A much easier task was researching the speeches made in Parliament and the actions taken by that body. Although the public reporting of the speeches of the members of Parliament was a punishable offense until 1774, auditors and spectators with shorthand skills from the gallery of the Commons could take down a speaker's words almost verbatim. These speeches eventually found their way into private journals, diaries, and letters. The speakers themselves felt no need to record their own words. Besides, what was said in both Houses of Parliament was for a long time a jealously guarded "privilege" which outsiders violated at their own peril. Further, most members of the Commons did not think themselves accountable to their electorates for their words or voting records.

But, to illustrate the benign dilemma in which I found myself, I will focus here on the circumstances surrounding Patrick Henry's Stamp Act Speech.

First, I will emphasize here that it was necessary to write Henry's speech, to compose it around the fragments and in a style that reflected Henry's character and recorded manner of speaking. The chief guide in this task was his "Give me liberty, or give me death" speech at St. John's Church in Richmond some ten years later, on the eve of war with Britain.

There are contradictory accounts of Henry's alleged "apology" to the House after he had been accused of treason by Speaker John Robinson. Lieutenant-Governor Francis Fauquier makes no mention of an apology in his subsequent report to the Board of Trade, nor does he dwell on the uproar in the House caused by the speech. If he meant to ingratiate himself with his superiors in London—he was always getting on their wrong side, especially on the matter of suspending clauses in

Virginia legislation he signed—he would certainly have mentioned it, and his friends in the House, Peyton Randolph, George Wythe, and others, would doubtless have told him about such an apology. But mention of it is conspicuously absent in Fauquier's report.

On the other hand, the anonymous Frenchman's account mentions an apology. Perhaps it was not an apology that the Frenchman heard, and he got it wrong. Apparently the session was a boisterous one, and the Frenchman, possibly a member of the minor French nobility in service to his government, was confused about what was happening and who was saying what. After all, the French *parlement* had not met in half a century.

Fauquier in his report also mentions that a copy of the Stamp Act had "crept into the house," but there is no evidence that the House ever had a copy of the Act at the time a protest to it was being debated, nor any evidence that any copies of it had reached North America in the spring of 1765. If a copy of the Act had been in the hands of the House, he certainly would have been loaned it to see what all the uproar was about. But in his report to the Board, there is not a single mention of any of its particulars. He would receive a copy of the Act long after it went into effect, November 1 of the same year.

Some accounts, including the anonymous Frenchman's, report that all seven Resolves were debated; others, only the first five. Fauquier implies that the sixth and seventh Resolves were in their advocates' "pocket" but were not discussed. That the fifth was erased from the journal record is a matter of fact. I anticipate this shameful action in the chapter set in the Commons, when Dogmael Jones's lone "nay" against the Stamp Act is nullified when a clerk is bribed to record the House vote as "unanimous."

How were Henry's Resolves—all seven of them, and not just the four that were passed by the House—broadcast to the other colonies, and so soon after their adoption? No one knows. Possibly Henry was responsible, but how? He was new to politics, and there is no evidence he was in correspondence with the editors and printers of colonial newspapers or in contact with other colonial representatives. Possibly one of his allies in the House undertook the task of copying out the

Resolves and sending them out. There is no evidence of that having happened, either. The Resolves certainly do not appear in the *Virginia Gazette* of the period, for the newspaper was more or less controlled by the Lieutenant-Governor, and the printer, Joseph Royle, a Tory, would not have been inclined to print them even had he the freedom to publish them.

All these gaps required decisions on how best to fill them. So, I wrote Henry's speech, recreated the debates, and saw to the broadcasting of the Resolves. Other gaps in the historical record were similarly exploited. The events, if they were integral to the story, were too important to neglect or gloss over.

Here I end my comments on this magnum opus. And here I shall repeat something I wrote in the acknowledgments in *Books One* and *Two*: I owe a debt of thanks to the Founders for having given me something worth writing about, and a country in which to write it.

1.   Ayn Rand, "What is Romanticism?" in *The Romantic Manifesto: A Philosophy of Literature,* revised edition (New York: Signet, 1975), 99.

2.   Ayn Rand, Introduction (1968) to *The Fountainhead*, (New York: Plume, 2005), vii.

3.   Ayn Rand, in *Ayn Rand Answers: The Best of Her Q&A*, Robert Mayhew, ed. (New York: New American Library, 2005), 188.

4.   Ayn Rand, "What is Romanticism?" 99.

5.   Edward Cline, *Sparrowhawk Book One: Jack Frake* (San Francisco: MacAdam/Cage, 2001), 148.

6.   *Pears Cyclopædia* (New York: Schocken Books, 1970), 13.

THE REVOLUTIONARIES

by Edward Cline

"Every idea needs a visible envelope, every principle needs a habitation," wrote Victor Hugo in his last novel, *Quatre-vingt-treize* (*Ninety-Three*),[1] set in the French Revolution during the Reign of Terror, published in 1874.

Hugo was writing about the first French Revolutionary Convention in Paris in September 1792. In this chapter he describes in meticulous detail the hall in which the Convention was held as a stage for drama. The hall was the "envelope" of that Convention, while *Ninety-Three*, the novel, itself is the "envelope" of an idea, postmarked 1793, but containing what Ayn Rand, who wrote an introduction to an edition of *Ninety-Three*, deems a story about "man's loyalty to values."

Rand would express nearly the same idea almost a century later: in fiction, ideas must be concretized. "Abstractions do not act."[2] Men act on ideas, and in fiction men must be concretized, as well, else they will be but moving abstractions, fuzzy, nearly invisible blueprints of characters never realized or sharply drawn, never anchored to specific, personal attributes of the writer's own creation, entities that are literarily incredible and unbelievable.

Hugo wrote in that introduction about the Convention: "Nothing loftier has ever appeared on mankind's horizon. There are the Himalayas and there is the Convention. The Convention may be history's highest point... It was through the Convention that the great new page was turned, and that the future of today began."

I love *Ninety-Three*, and have reread it many times. That statement, however, is one of the few in the novel I have ever taken issue with. When I encounter it, a question invariably pops into my mind: And not the American Revolution? Was it not the loftiest event in human history? Was not the American Revolution a great new turn of the page of history, and the foundation of what would be the future of the world? The American Revolution was a success, the French a catastrophic failure. The American Revolution was radical, without precedent in history; the French, antiradical, and precedented in the past, when mobs and the "majority" established tyrannies in ancient Rome and Greece. The French sought to emulate the American Revolution, but ended with the Reign of Terror and an emperor. The American Revolution sought to grant men "life, liberty, and the pursuit of happiness," and largely kept that promise up until the end of the nineteenth century. The French Revolution promised "liberty, equality, and fraternity," but, obsessed with an "equality" rooted in envy and collectivism, it denied men both liberty and the fraternity possible to and among free men, and collapsed almost immediately into a new despotism.

Imagine it: If the American Revolution had failed—if Britain had suppressed the revolt of her colonies against tyranny, or if George Washington had succumbed to temptation to become George the First, the American king, as many wished him to—would not have the interminable warfare between rival powers continued well into the nineteenth century? The French Revolution, which may not have happened without the example of the American, was followed by the dictatorship of Napoleon, whose quest for empire led to a clash with Britain, a clash that did not end until 1815 and Waterloo.

But, Hugo can be forgiven his exclusionary pride in France. It would be churlish and presumptuous to belabor it. He was as much a patriot as he was a novelist. His evaluation of France's history is not off the mark. At the beginning of that same chapter, where he comments on how men viewed the Convention, he writes: "One has a strange feeling: aversion to the great. One sees the abysses without seeing the sublimities. Thus was the Convention judged at first. It was examined by nearsighted men when it was made to be contemplated by eagles."[3]

Hugo died in 1885, and as his country mourned his passing, Frédéric-Auguste Bartholdi's Statue of Liberty, a gift from a friendly and grateful France, was being erected in New York Harbor. It is almost as though France were making a present to America of the soul of her greatest patriot and novelist.

"To a Romanticist, a background is a background, not a theme. His vision is always focused on man—on the fundamentals of man's nature, on those problems and aspects of his character which apply to any age and any country."[4] The British-American politics and culture of the eighteenth century are thus a background to the principal heroes of *Sparrowhawk*, but the ideas and principles that moved them are ageless, as applicable in that century as they are in this one. If the men who made the Revolution possible had not been "real," there would have been no Revolution. It is such "reality" that I wished to make credible and "real," as "visible" and credible as Hugo's heroes were to him.

Sparrowhawk is an "envelope" of ideas, of principles, of men acting on those ideas and principles. It fills a gap in American literature about why the American Revolution happened, and presents the caliber of men who made it possible. It is about their discovery, in the characters of Jack Frake, Hugh Kenrick, and in a handful of other minor heroes, of ideas that were compatible with their existence as men who thought and acted for their own sakes and own reasons, and not from duty or loyalty to the Crown.

There have been numerous novels set in the pre-Revolutionary period. Most of them are little more than costume dramas. Their characters are twentieth–century men, imposters wearing eighteenth-century apparel, transported to a century alien to them in spirit, stature, and action. They are too recognizable and so not credible. If one is searching for a clue to why the men of the Revolution did what they did and thought what they thought, it is exasperating or confusing to encounter in fiction the kinds of men one is familiar with in one's own time, men to whom the Founders' moral stature, intelligence, and capacity for action are impossible.

Likewise incredible are those novels in which the primary characters are unrealized abstractions that expound the ideas of the Revolution. One wants to like them, or praise them, but their unreality prohibits their concretization, and as a consequence, the ideas and events of the Revolution also remain unreal and one develops no affection for them.

Cimourdain, Gauvain, Lantenac—the giants who move *Ninety-Three*, are credible, arresting, convincing characters integrated in a three-way conflict rarely matched in literature in the plotting and climax of the novel (except by Rand herself in *We the Living*, *The Fountainhead*, and *Atlas Shrugged*). All three could be said to be uncompromisingly idealistic and moved solely by their ideals: Lantenac, the ruthless royalist, by his vision of a restored monarchy; Cimourdain and Gauvain, the dedicated republicans, by opposing spirits of the Revolution.

But, as Rand noted in her introduction, Hugo was not able to imbue his giants with credible, convincing intellects. "His fire, his eloquence, his emotional power seemed to desert him when he had to deal with theoretical subjects."[5] Thus, the political dialogue between these three seems flat and stale when compared with the rest of the novel (although that dialogue is in another literary galaxy when compared with what passes for modern political discourse, in fiction and in real life). Given Hugo's less-than-grand polemics in the novel that were responsible for a momentous event (including the acerbic, yet oddly vapid exchanges between Marat, Danton, and Robespierre earlier in the novel), and he understood the French Revolution at least as well as did its actual provocateurs, it is little wonder that the French Revolution failed.

One task in writing the *Sparrowhawk* novels was to project the growth of the ideas behind the Revolution in its heroes, to make the ideas as real and credible as the heroes. This meant introducing the principal heroes, Jack Frake and Hugh Kenrick, at a period of their lives when ideas would have an almost immediate influence on them, and when their hold on their own lives and identities as independent beings was most crucial. Because they refuse to surrender those things, they are able to proceed, step by step, to each stage of maturation to become independent, self-contained men.

That task complemented the task of rendering all the characters, especially Frake and Kenrick, credible representatives of the ideas they represented or expounded, and to bring those ideas to life, as well. The degree to which readers of the series have expressed an emotional attachment (or revulsion) to these characters, is a measure of the success in making those characters real. To elicit an emotional, personal response to a character in a reader is also a measure of how convincing that character is. It reveals another thing, as well: the character of the reader himself.

Hugo wrote about the Convention: "These were all tragedies begun by giants and finished by dwarfs."[6] Elsewhere, he observed: "When greatness is a crime, it is a sign of the reign of the little."[7]

America today is being finished off by such dwarfs, in philosophy, in politics, in the arts, and especially in literature. The dwarfs are nearsighted and wish to reduce everyone to their epistemological state and to share their subjectivist or nihilistic metaphysics. They assert that since none of the Founders was "perfect"—since Washington and Jefferson and Patrick Henry owned slaves, for example—then America is flawed, if not founded on fraud, fabrication, or myth, and so the ideas that inspired its origins are therefore dishonest, invalid, or arbitrary, and may be discarded.

This is the modern method of argumentation and persuasion: to attack the ideas by attacking the man, and presumably discredit the ideas as well as the man. It could be called refutation through irrelevancies. Most modern readers are inured to such circuitous sleights-of-mind, otherwise known as sophistry, having encountered little else in their education, in politics, or in the press.

It is such dishonesty and nearsightedness, promulgated by those intellectual dwarfs, especially in our universities, that I wished to correct and banish by offering an epic of giants (chiefly to preserve my own sanity, and as a vehicle of justice to the men of the Revolution), by arming a reader with an eagle's perspective on the Revolution, to inculcate a vision of man not possible in the choking swamp fog of modern culture. *Sparrowhawk*, a novel written in an age when such epics are disdained by the intellectual and literary establishment, has enjoyed a success measured by its enthusiastic reception by a reading public desperate for relief from modern subjectivism and in search of reason, a success that renders the odds against the novel's appearance and value irrelevant. That success has been personally encouraging and gratifying.

The series is, to borrow the title of a Terence Rattigan play about another hero, my "bequest to the nation." It was my "mistress" for thirteen years; I denied it nothing and devoted most of my conscious hours to researching and writing it. *Book Six: War* was finished in the spring of 2005. It has been difficult to begin another literary project, such as a third Roaring Twenties detective novel, my having completed the first two novels of that genre before beginning *Sparrowhawk*. Researching and recreating the 1920s served as training to investigate and recreate the eighteenth century.

Sparrowhawk is my fourth series, for a total of fifteen novels. *Sparrowhawk* itself is over two thousand pages or some seven million words in length. When I create a hero, I cannot let him go until I have developed him to his fullest. And when I reach that point, then his story is complete. There will be no further Merritt Fury or Chess Hanrahan adventures or cases; perhaps there will be a third Cyrus Skeen novel, ending, appropriately, with the stock market crash of 1929.

1. Victor Hugo, *Ninety-Three,* Lowell Bair, trans. (New York: Bantam, 1962), 122.

2. Ayn Rand, *The Art of Fiction: A Guide for Writers and Readers*, Tore Boeckmann, ed. (New York: Plume, 2000), 53.

3. Hugo, *Ninety-Three,* 122.

4. Ayn Rand, Introduction to *Ninety-Three*, Lowell Bair, trans.

5. Ayn Rand, Introduction to *Ninety-Three*, Lowell Bair, trans.

6. Hugo, *Ninety-Three*, 122.

7. Victor Hugo in "Genius and Taste," from his "Postscriptum de Ma Vie," in *Victor Hugo's Intellectual Autobiography*, Lorenzo O'Rourke, trans. (New York: Funk & Wagnalls Company, 1907).

LACUNÆ AND ARTISTIC LICENSE

by Edward Cline

[**lacuna** *n.* (*pl.* ~ **æ** *or* ~ **as**). Hiatus, blank, missing portion
(esp. in ancient MS., book, etc.; empty part.)
—*Concise Oxford Dictionary*]

Someone may ask about *Sparrowhawk*: If one of my purposes were to recreate a world of heroes and the era that saw the birth of the United States, how can one create one's own world in a historical novel, when one's characters must conform to the historical record?

The answer is: When there is no historical record for them to conform to. Moreover, the question is asked on the premise that it is impossible to recreate a historical period and also write a Romantic novel in which the characters exercise volition and can choose and pursue their values in that period. It certainly is an achievable literary goal, and *Sparrowhawk* sets no precedent in this regard. Victor Hugo, Sir Walter Scott, Alexandre Dumas (père) and other nineteenth–century novelists and playwrights did it without risking the charge that they rewrote history.

And, there is a certain irrelevancy to the question. One doesn't choose to write a Romantic-historical novel solely to recreate a particular period. One may as well write a history. If the period is important to one's fiction-writing purposes—and certainly the pre-Revolutionary period in the American colonies and Britain was integral to mine—then the characters one creates must be able to act freely in it, just as they should in a story set in one's own time.

In writing *Sparrowhawk*, it was important for me to heed and respect the historical record, because my characters are depicted as contributing to some of the events of the time. In recreating the events in the Virginia General Assembly and the House of Commons, for example, it was crucial that they be portrayed objectively and in character. This meant availing myself of the extant records and journals of both institutions.

And in those records and journals I discovered significant gaps. Of course, there were no such members of the Commons as Dogmael Jones and Henoch Pannell, no rotten boroughs as Swansditch and Canovan. On this side of the Atlantic, there was no such county as Queen Anne in Virginia, and no burgesses by the names of Hugh Kenrick and Edgar Cullis to represent it in the General Assembly. The boroughs, county, and characters are all pure creations.

But, it was not a journalistic, naturalistic novel I wished to write. The gaps in the historical record made it easier for me to recreate the culture and politics of the period in Romantic terms, and to fill those gaps with my story. As Ayn Rand noted in her Introduction to Hugo's *Ninety-Three*, "To a Romanticist, a background is just a background, not a theme. His vision is always focused on man—on the fundamentals of man's nature, on those problems and aspects of his character which apply to any age and any country."[1] A background is similar to a theatrical setting, a stage on which men may think and act in a plotted story. The props, the costumes, the lighting, and so on, are all a means of establishing time and place, merely "special effects" subsumed by the story. (Today, special effects in film and on the stage are becoming the dominant focus, at the expense of the story, when there is one.)

While the records of Parliament in *Sparrowhawk*'s period are abundant (though still incomplete), there is a paucity of records of the General Assembly, and what exists of them is colorless and dry, thick with the yawn-inducing minutiæ of mundane, unimportant issues. On the other hand, in reading the accounts of the debates in Parliament on the Stamp Act, one encounters a startling mix of eloquence and rude manners, unbridled passion and sly connivance.

Where the record was incomplete, I relied on secondary sources, such as diaries, letters, and newspaper accounts to reconstruct events.

Even then, I had to fall back on my deductive powers and imagination when the records were lacking or so vague or sketchy as to be useless. For example, the numbers of the *Virginia Gazette*, published in Williamsburg, that might have reported what actually happened in the General Assembly in May 1765 when Patrick Henry introduced his Resolves, are missing. Furthermore, I found that I had to write Henry's "Cæsar had his Brutus" speech, because there is no written record of it, only memorable fragments recalled by men years after the event.

Let me cite two important events: the debates on the Stamp Act in Parliament, and the debates over the Stamp Act Resolves in the General Assembly, dramatized in *Book Four: Empire*.

Many of the actual speeches made by George Grenville, Isaac Barré, and other actual members of the Commons are excerpted in the novel. The two major fictive speeches made by Dogmael Jones and Henoch Pannell represent the fundamental, opposing positions taken by the parties; Pannell's an expression of contempt for the colonies, Jones's a spirited defense of them. But, the climax of the debates was the vote on the Stamp Act. The record shows that it was unanimous, with no dissenting votes noted.

Jones, of course, would have voted against the Act, and his would have been the single, lone dissent. To "conform" to the actual record, and to underscore the venality rife in the Commons at that time, I have Grenville's secretary bribe the House clerk not to record Jones's dissenting vote in the official journal.

Hugh Kenrick calls the General Assembly a "cameo" of Parliament. Complementing the absence of Jones's dissenting vote in the Commons journal was the subsequent expunction of Patrick Henry's fifth Resolve, and probably the sixth and seventh, as well, from the Burgesses's journal. There are contradictory accounts on whether or not the sixth and seventh were even introduced, debated, and voted on, one by an anonymous Frenchman who witnessed the debates, the other by Lieutenant-Governor Francis Fauquier in his official report to the Board of Trade in London.

The contradictory accounts create a unique lacuna. Which account is true? Whose veracity, the Frenchman's or the Lieutenant-Governor's, should one place more weight on? Without any supporting evidence one way or the other, and in this instance there is none, it is anyone's edu-

cated guess about what actually happened. One would think that such
an epochal event would have been meticulously documented. But, either
it was not, or if it was, the records perished, or are molding undiscov-
ered in someone's attic or in some library's special collections.

The greater gap was the means by which all seven of Henry's
Resolves were broadcast to colonial newspapers outside of Virginia.
There is no record of who was responsible for sending them. Henry at
that time was a freshman burgess for his county, and it is doubtful that
he knew any of the editors of those newspapers. Accounts of the event
and biographies of the principal actors simply gloss over the subject.
(My own unsupported theory is that it was Richard Henry Lee, burgess
for Westmoreland County, who, because of the animus between him and
the conservative Tidewater gentry that controlled the House, was not
present during the Resolves debates that spring but who published his
own protest of the Stamp Act.)

The Resolves, to our knowledge, were not reported in the *Virginia
Gazette*, which was controlled by the Lieutenant-Governor, who dissolved the Assembly over the Resolves. The numbers of the *Gazette*
from that period are missing. Perhaps one of Henry's allies in the House
was responsible. The evidence of responsibility is simply absent. So, I hit
upon a means for the Resolves to be sent "abroad."

It was important that I devise a means of disseminating the
Resolves, for they served to unite the colonies for the first time in a
common cause, which was to challenge Parliamentary authority. I date
the true beginning of the Revolution to the summer of 1765.

Let us examine Patrick Henry's Stamp Act Speech as I dramatize it
in *Book Four: Empire* of *Sparrowhawk* together with a historian's
account of the actual event. I will use excerpts from Carl Bridenbaugh's
Seat of Empire: The Political Role of Eighteenth Century Williamsburg
(1950, Colonial Williamsburg Press, pp. 60-65).

Bridenbaugh writes that an anonymous Frenchman reports his
arrival [from York County] in the House of Burgesses just as Patrick
Henry rose to deliver his "Cæsar had his Brutus" speech. The
Frenchman claims in his diary that Henry apologized for his remarks to
Speaker Robinson. However, there is no reason to ascribe any veracity

or accuracy to his report, especially since he did not report important episodes during the debates. For example, he reports that the sixth and seventh Resolves were "hotly debated," although Lieutenant-Governor Fauquier claims they were not debated. Who is to be believed?

Bridenbaugh writes, "They [either Henry and his House allies, or just his allies] carefully saw to it that copies of the four recorded Resolves plus the one expunged and the two withheld were sent to Philadelphia correspondents for use where they would do the most good. From this metropolis they were dispatched by water to Rhode Island, and six of them made their first appearance in Samuel Hall's *Newport Mercury* for June 24, 1765." Who was responsible? There is no record of responsibility extant. The *Boston Gazette* on July 1, together with other colonial newspapers, printed all seven Resolves.

Bridenbaugh's entire account of the session of May 1765 is skeptical, if not deprecatory, of virtually every fact he presents in it, especially when he discusses Henry. But his account is but one of several I consulted while putting together the data to write Chapter 9: The Resolves, in Part Two of *Book Four*.

One possible reason that no one living then claimed responsibility for disseminating the Resolves to the other colonies is that he could have been charged with treason or sedition by the Crown. If Samuel Hall of the *Newport Mercury* received signed correspondence from the party or parties who sent him the Resolves, it has not survived. If it had survived, this and other gaps in the historical record would have been filled, and we would have more conclusive knowledge of what happened.

Fans of the *Sparrowhawk* series have pleaded with me to continue it, but they must be content with its fiery conclusion on the York River in September of 1775. I accomplished in the last chapters of *Book Six* what I had set out to do. One can imagine that the epic could be extended indefinitely, but to attempt that would be, for me, a pointless anticlimax and a violation of the story's integrity. As it stands, in terms of its plot and theme, the series goes full circle to its beginnings in *Books One* and *Two*.

1. Victor Hugo, *Ninety-Three,* Lowell Bair, trans. (New York: Bantam, 1962), xi-xii.

SPARROWHAWK CHARACTER, SHIP,
AND PLANTATION STAFF LISTS

Compiled by Edward Cline

At the beginning of *Book One*, Parson Robert Parmley advises young Jack Frake: "If ever you must choose a name or symbol for something important, think on it most earnestly."

I heeded his advice. One of the pleasanter research tasks of *Sparrowhawk* was the creation of over 370 character and place names. The etymological root meaning of Jack's surname is "man warrior," from the Old English "freake," which in turn meant a man who was exceptional or outstanding. Friends have remarked that *Frake* is too harsh sounding. But harshness is what I sought; the harsher, or blunter the name, the more memorable it would be. The root meaning of Hugh Kenrick's surname is "man hero." Researching and choosing their names from among a dozen candidates required my best attention, because they are the principal heroes of the series; I needed to be comfortable working with them over the course of what would become the approximately seven million words in the series.

Most of the names of the principal characters required nearly the same degree of attention and selectivity, chosen from a long list of candidates I compiled chiefly from ships' passenger rosters of the eighteenth century, and many from other sources. Most of the character and place names in the series are contemporaneous with the eighteenth century. When I could not find a character name I was happy with, I invented one; and if the invented name were not strictly contemporaneous, then it had to be credibly so.

For space reasons, I cannot discuss the root meanings or associations of all 370 names, so I will highlight only a handful here. Many of the characters appear in only one or two *Books*; others occur in all six.

First, about some place names. To my knowledge, no such place as *Onyxcombe* exists in England. The name of Crispin Hillier's constituency in Dorset is a combination of a precious stone, "onyx," and "combe," Old English for a kind of coastal valley. Too late did I realize, by the time I had finished writing *Book Two*, that I had intruded upon Thomas Hardy country by inventing a town, a river, and an aristocracy to alter the makeup of the shire of Dorset; they are as fictive as Hardy's "Wessex." See young Hugh Kenrick's description of his ancestral part of Dorset in Chapter 11 of *Book Two*. While researching the towns and topography of Cornwall, I chanced upon a town called "Morvel." I changed it to *Marvel*; my subconscious kept translating *Morvel* to "morbid village" and the connotation did not agree with me. *Gwynnford* is an adaptation of the name of the hero in Victor Hugo's *The Man Who Laughs*.

The rotten borough of *Swansditch* in London across old London Bridge adjacent to Southwark is also nonexistent. Dogmael Jones neatly presents its history and etymology near the end of *Book Three*. The fictive rotten borough of *Canovan,* once Augustus Skelly's and appropriated by Henoch Pannell, is a borrowing from an earlier (unpublished) suspense novel of mine. *Lion Key*, first mentioned in *Book Two*, sits in an evidentiary purgatory. Maps of mid-eighteenth-century London show a number of keys or wharves in the Pool of London, and all but one could be accounted for in terms of their past owners. Records for Lion Key were not extant, however; its ownership proved untraceable. Lion Key came into the possession of Benjamin Worley and Sons, commercial agents of the Kenrick family.

Personal names. *Etáin* means "shining one"; what better name for the future romantic interest of my heroes? *Reverdy* was initially a problem. I encountered the name only once, on a passenger roster. Usually such rosters featured an emigrant's name, followed by a trade or profession. *Reverdy* appeared by itself, with no trade or profession appended to it. At first sight, it struck me as an eminently feminine name, rich in connotation, and so it became one. *Dogmael* is a distinctive name, as well, Welsh meaning "bringer of light to children." What more appropriate name for a barrister who attempts to introduce reason and justice into his court cases and speaks eloquently for them in the chamber of the House of Commons, packed as it was with a few hundred dimly lit members?

Redmagne? I encountered this name only once, as well, in my voluminous reading of eighteenth–century pamphlets, newspapers, and screeds. *Glorious Swain* explains his name to young Hugh Kenrick in *Book Two*, and the origin of John *Proudlocks* occurs in *Book Three*. *Effney* is my personal variation on *Ethne*, the name of the romantic interest in A.E.W. Mason's *The Four Feathers*.

The villains. In selecting these names I relied more on euphony, rhythm, and connotation than on etymology. Their names had to be memorably distasteful. Thus, for example, *Jared Turley*, the Earl's bastard son and long arm of malice, and *Alden Curle*, the fawning, secretly sneering butler and major domo of Windridge Court. As for *Claybourne*, the Earl's suffering but obsequious personal valet, I trust his name needs no explication. *Pannell*'s root meaning is "pain"; what tax collector and supporter of oppressive legislation isn't one?

Across the ocean in Caxton, Virginia, there is *Albert Acland*, an Anglican cleric acridly hostile to all things revolutionary. The reader never meets *Amos Swart*, the slovenly, careless former owner of Brougham Hall, bought and salvaged by Hugh Kenrick and renamed Meum Hall. There was a wealth of slave names to choose from, many of them of obvious or probable African origin, such as *Bilico, Dilch,* and *Benabe*.

I did not intend writing a *roman à clef*, but *Sparrowhawk* abounds with subtle tributes to favorite individuals and things. I leave most of them to a literary scholar to discover and reveal, if such a project is ever undertaken. These names represent not only characters, but also places and even ships. They might refer to a personal friend, a favorite play, novel, or author, to a character in a novel or movie. This was a practice I began with my very first (unpublished) novel and have continued without guilt or regret ever since. A few of these "namesakes" are fairly obvious, and the individuals they salute know who they are. Most, however, are more or less disguised. *Morland*, for example, was once James Bond's preferred brand of cigarette, while *Meservy* also has its origins in the Fleming novels. *Winslow* LeGrand's name reveals my appreciation for Terence Rattigan's plays, and Nathan *Rickerby* can thank Mickey Spillane for his place in *Book Two*. *Hillier* and *Kemp* are taken from H.G. Wells's *The Time Machine*, the first novel I ever read (after seeing director George Pal's 1960 version of it), and which ignited my intellectual curiosity about the world I lived in.

Ship names were also a pleasure to create. Many that appear in the series were of actual warships of the period, such as the *Rainbow*, *Fowey*, and *Diligence*, stationed in Hampton Roads. The merchantmen *Roilance* and *Galvin*, though, are purely fictive, and are the namesakes of two modern British composers. There was a *Sparrow-Hawk* warship in the seventeenth century—it ran aground off Cape Cod—but my *Sparrowhawk* owes its name to the Curtis Sparrowhawk fighter-reconnaissance biplanes of the Navy and Army Air Corp in the first half of the twentieth century. It is noteworthy that in the Age of Enlightenment merchant and naval vessels were given names either from Greek or Roman mythology and history, or names indigenous to the eighteenth century. Thus Skelly's original merchant ship, the *Pegasus*, before his outlaw career, and his smuggling ship, *The Hasty Hart*, adapted from the title of a play by John Patrick.

There are "cameo" appearances by actual historical persons in the series, e.g., the Duke of Cumberland, George Grenville, William Pitt, and Lord Chesterfield, as well as by Thomas Jefferson, George Washington, Patrick Henry, and Peyton Randolph. They are not in the story merely to lend it color or authenticity; if they speak and act in it, they contribute to the plot. Are their characterizations true and accurate? I discuss this subject in the Foreword to this volume.

Readers might note that the one person who does not appear in the series is George the Third. Historically, the monarch did not become an object of general colonial enmity until just after the battle of Bunker or Breed's Hill in June 1775. Up to the beginning of armed conflict, patriots, including many signers of the Declaration of Independence, were toasting his health and wishing him and his family well. The toasts ceased, once blood had been spilled. But, all along, from 1763 onward, he merely reacted to Parliament's designs and legislation. He was not so much a mover or cause of the events as he was a filigreed rubber stamp; hardly a speaking role, and, try as I might, I could not find a more active role for him in the story, except in narrative.

The lists that follow became necessary when, after finishing *Book Two*, I began to lose track of or misplace characters and even ships. The population of *Sparrowhawk*'s universe swelled when the series' setting first moved from England to the York River in Virginia in *Book Three,* and then in subsequent *Books* when I filled the benches of the House of Commons and the House of Burgesses in Williamsburg with friends and enemies of liberty. Most of the names in the first list are of characters who actually appear in the series; a handful are of characters who appear "off stage," such as Amos Swart in *Book Three* and Captain Musto of the ill-fated *Charon* near the end of *Book Two*.

So, like Jack Frake, I heeded Parson Parmley's advice to think earnestly on the names I chose for my characters, places, and ships. It is the only advice from a cleric I have ever taken seriously.

NAME	ROLE AND BOOK NUMBER
Abingdon, Earl (4th)	Willoughby Montagu Bertie, pro-American—Book 5
Acland, Albert	Pastor, Stepney Parish, Caxton—Books 3-6
Albertoli, Sig.	Hugh's fencing master—Book 2
Ambrose, Charles	Skelly Gang—Book 1
Anderson, Clough	Clerk, General Assembly—Book 4
Ashton, Mr.	Justice, Falmouth trial—Book 1
Autt, Francis	Scullion, Sea Siren—Book 1
Ayre, William	Skelly Gang—Book 1
Bailey, Idonea	Housekeeper, Morland Hall—Books 3-4
Barré, Isaac	MP for Chipping Wycombe, later for Calne—Books 4-5
Barret, Travis	Wendel Barret's nephew—Books 5-6
Barret, Wendel	Publisher, Caxton *Courier*—Books 3-5
Beck, Israel	Husband of Mary, Morland Hall—Books 4-6

Beck, Mary   Cook, Morland Hall—Books 3-6

Beckford, William   MP for London—Books 4-5

Beckwith, Col.   71st Foot, Hulton's original regiment—Books 2-3

Beecroft, Rupert   Business Agent, Meum Hall, Caxton—Books 3-6

Benabe   Slave, Meum Hall—Book 3

Berkeley, Norbonne   Baron Botetourt, Lt.-Governor—Book 6

Biddle, John   Worley Partner, Lion Key—Book 2

Bigelow, Timothy   Tenant, Morland Hall—Book 3

Bilico   Slave, Meum Hall—Book 3

Binns, Mr.   Falmouth gaoler—Book 1

Blackstone, William   MP for Hindon, legal scholar—Book 5

Blair, John   President of Gov. Council—Books 4-5

Blair, Matthew   A.K.A. Redmagne—Book 1

Bland, Richard   Burgess, Prince George, General Assembly—Books 4-6

Blassard, Mr.   Revenue Man, crony of Hunt—Book 6

Blevins   Family of Londontown, Maryland—Book 2

Blissom, Brice   Marquis of Bilbury, son of Guthlac—Book 2

Blissom, Guthlac   Marquis of Bilbury—Book 2

Brashears, Beverly   Pippin: Elspeth/Electra—Book 2

Bridgette, Miss   Governess, maid—Books 2-3

Bristol   Apprentice, slave, Meum Hall—Book 3

Brompton, Peter   Pippin: Steven/Sterope—Book 2

Brougham, Covington   Past owner of Brougham/Meum Hall—Book 3

Brown, William   Ferrymaster, Londontown, Maryland—Book 3

Brune, James   Brother of Reverdy—Books 2-6

Brune, Mrs.   Wife of Robert—Book 2

Brune, Reverdy   Daughter of Robert—Books 2-6

Brune, Robert   Squire, neighbor of the Kenricks in Dorset—Book 2

Buckle, Henry   Reisdale's cooper, Caxton—Book 5

Burke, Edmund   MP for Wendover, Bristol, Rockinghamite—Books 5-6

Camden, Baron   Charles Pratt, Chief Justice, Common Pleas—Book 5

Carrington, Paul   Burgess, Charlotte, General Assembly—Book 4

Carter, Landon   Burgess, Richmond County, General Assembly—Book

Cary, Mr.   Gwynnford merchant—Book 1

Cavie, Mr.   Instructor, Dr. Comyn's School—Book 2

Chance, Fiona	Cook, Meum Hall—Book 3
Chandler, Brice	A.K.A. Redmagne—Book 1
Cheney, Mr.	Captain, *Ariadne*—Book 1
Chiswell, John	Burgess, Williamsburg, General Assembly—Books 4-5
Claxon, Richard	Skelly Gang—Book 1
Claybourne	Basil Kenrick's valet—Books 2-6
Cletus	Wendel Barret's apprentice slave—Books 5-6
Cole, Adeline	Actress—Book 1
Cole, Mr.	Hugh's tutor—Book 2
Colewort	Marquis of, Guest at Pumphrett House—Book 2
Comyn, Dr. James	Headmaster, Comyn's School, London—Book 2
Cooke, George	MP for Middlesex—Book 5
Corbin, Jewel	Wife of Moses—Book 3
Corbin, Moses	Mayor of Caxton—Books 3-6
Corsin, Enolls	Business Agent, Sachem Hall—Book 6
Cottle, Mr.	Bookshop owner—Book 2
Craun, Mr.	Revenue man—Book 1
Crisp, Vivian	A.K.A. Redmagne—Book 1
Crofts, Charles	Captain, 6th Marine Battalion—Book 6
Croisset, Alphonse	French commercial agent—Books 3-4
Crompton, Aymer	Brickmaker, Morland Hall—Books 3-6
Cruger, Henry	MP for Bristol—Book 6
Cullis, Edgar	Son of Ralph, Burgess for Queen Anne—Books 3-6
Cullis, Eleanor	Daughter of Ralph—Book 3
Cullis, Hetty	Wife of Ralph—Books 3-6
Cullis, Ralph	Planter, Caxton—Books 3-6
Cumberland	William Augustus, Duke of, son of George II—Books 1-2
Cupid	Jefferson's slave—Book 4
Curle, Alden	Basil Kenrick's butler, major domo—Books 2-6
Cust, John	MP for Grantham, Speaker of Commons—Books 4-5
Dakin, Henry	Tenant, Morland Hall—Books 3-6
Dakin, Ruth	Servant, wife of Henry, Morland Hall—Books 3-6
Darling, Jack	A.K.A. Redmagne—Book 1
Dawson, A.	Printer/bookseller—Book 1
Delia	Slave, Meum Hall—Book 3

Dent, Jasper	Leith's cousin—Book 1
Deverix, James	Peruker/Barber—Book 3
Dilch	Slave, Meum Hall—Books 3-6
Doherty, Tom	Powder monkey, *Sparrowhawk*—Book 6
Dolman, Horace	Steward, Windridge Court—Book 2
Doody, Tim	Serving boy, Fruit Wench—Book 2
Dorn, Arthur	Student, Inns of Court—Book 5
Driscoll, Sawny	Pen name of Brashears—Book 2
Eales, Bernard	Captain, *Ariadne*—Books 3-4
Easley, Israel	Brother of Novus—Book 3
Easley, Novus	Philadelphia Quaker/Merchant—Books 3-5
Edgecombe, Armiger	King's Proctor—Book 1
Effingham, Earl (3rd)	Thomas Howard, pro-American—Book 5
Embry, Mr.	Merchant—Book 1
Farbrace, Timothy	Naval officer, *Rover, Zeus*—Books 1-2
Fauquier, Francis	Lt.-Governor of Virginia, 1758-68—Books 3-5
Faure, Bamber	Vicar of St. Thraille's—Book 2
Fawkner, Everard	Duke of Cumberland's aide—Book 2
Ferguson, William	Clerk, General Assembly—Book 4
Fern, Joshua	Fern's Tavern—Books 3, 5, 6
Fineux, John	Skelly Gang—Book 1
Fix, Mr.	Revenue man—Book 1
Fleming, John	Burgess, Cumberland, General Assembly—Book 4
Fletcher, John	William's son—Book 5
Fletcher, William	Ironmonger, Barret's in-law—Book 5
Formby, George	Kenrick banking partner—Book 2
Frake, Cephas	Father of Jack—Book 1
Frake, Huldah	Mother of Jack—Book 1
Frake, Jack	All Books
Franklin, Benjamin	Colonial agent (London)—Books 4-5
Frazer, Jock	Planter—Books 5-6
Frew, Oswald	Leith's attorney (Falmouth)—Book 1
Fuller, Rose	MP for Maidstone—Book 5
Gage, Gen. Thomas	Cmdr-in-Chief, British. Army, No. America—Book 6
Galpin, Mr.	Hugh's tutor—Book 2

Gammage, Peter	A.K.A. Redmagne—Book 1
Gandy, Mary	Edgar Cullis's cousin—Book 4
Garth, Charles	MP for Devizes—Book 4
Gascoyne, Bamber	MP for Midhurst, barrister—Book 5
Geary, Elyot	Captain, *Sparrowhawk*—Books 5-6
George I	Lewis, or Ludwig, grandfather of George III
Giddens, Dorsey	Tenant farmer, Meum Hall—Book 3-6
Goostrey, Sir Miles	Under-secretary of state—Book 2
Gould, Mr.	Friend of William Horlick—Book 2
Grainger, Sir Bevil	Master of the Rolls, King's Bench, Pippin Trial, later Viscount of Wooten & Clarence—Books 2-5
Gramatan, Carver	Gramatan Inn, Caxton—Books 3-6
Granby, Damaris	Wife of Ira, Caxton—Books 3-4
Granby, Ira	Planter, Caxton—Book 3-4
Granby, Selina	Daughter of Ira, marries James Vishonn—Books 3-4
Granby, William	Son of Ira, Burgess, Caxton, marries Eleanor Cullis—Book 4
Greene, Richard	Skelly Gang—Book 1
Grenville, George	MP for Buckingham, Prime Minister—Books 4-5
Griffin, Mary	Serving wench, Gramatan Inn—Book 6
Grimby, Mr.	Grimby, Holtby & Brizard Bank—Book 2
Grynsmith, Humphrey	Sheriff, Falmouth—Book 1
Hamlyn, John	Bully, Green Park, London—Book 2
Hanway, Mr.	Danvers warden—Book 2
Harke, James	Lieutenant, British Navy, *Rainbow*—Book 5
Harle, Sir Francis E.	Rear Admiral—Books 1-2
Harris, James	MP for Christchurch—Book 5
Harris, Maud	Duke of Cumberland's mistress—Book 2
Haslam, Simon	Prosecutor, Skelly trial—Book 1
Haynie, Mr.	*Sparrowhawk*'s bursar—Book 2
Heathcoate, Lydia	Seamstress, Caxton—Books 3-6
Henry	Cooper, slave, Morland Hall—Book 3
Henry, Patrick	Burgess, Louisa, General Assembly—Book 4
Herbert, Mr.	MP for Ruxton—Book 2
Hewitt, James	MP for Coventry—Book 5

Hillier, Crispin	MP for Onyxcombe—Books 2-6
Hockaday, Geoffrey	Son of Nicholas—Book 1
Hockaday, Nicholas	Marquis of Epping—Book 1
Hogue, Richard	Theater producer—Book 5
Holets, Capt. James	MP for Oakhead Abbas—Book 5
Horlick, William	Pippin: Mathius/Merope—Book 2
Hosphus, Mr.	Cornwall fisherman—Book 1
Howard, George	MP for Lostwithiel, Major General (pro-American)—Book 4
Huggens, Oswald	Magistrate, Common Pleas—Book 2
Hulton, Thomas	Hugh's valet—Books 2, 3, 6
Hunt, Jared	Turley's alias, bastard son of Earl of Danvers—Books 4-6
Hunter, Thomas	MP for Winchelsea—Book 4
Hurry, William	Overlooker—Morland Hall—Book 3
Huske, John	MP for Malden—Book 5
Ingoldsby, Robert	Late MP for Swansditch—Book 3
Innes, James	Captain, Williamsburg Volunteers—Book 5
Iverson, Mr.	*Sparrowhawk*'s surgeon—Book 2
Ivy, Richard	Tobacco inspector, Caxton—Book 3
Jeamer, Jeremy	Jack Frake's "London" alias—Book 1
Jefferson, Thomas	Burgess, Albemarle, law student—Books 4-6
Jenyns, Soame	MP for Cambridge Borough—Book 4
Johnson, Samuel	Writer, lexicographer—Books 2-6
Johnston, George	Burgess, Fairfax, General Assembly—Book 4
Jones, Sir Dogmael	Serjeant-at-law, barrister, King's Bench, later MP for Swansditch—Books 2-5
Kemp, Mr.	MP for Harbin—Book 2
Kennaway, Ian	Captain, merchant sloop *Morag*—Book 5
Kenny, Jude	Brother of Will—Books 3-6
Kenny, Will	Brother of Jude—Books 3-6
Kenrick, Alice	Sister of Hugh—Books 2-6
Kenrick, Basil	15th Earl of Danvers—Books 2-6
Kenrick, Effney	Baroness of Danvers, mother of Hugh—Books 2-6
Kenrick, Garnet	Baron of Danvers, father of Hugh, brother of Basil—

	Books 2-6
Kenrick, Guy	14th Earl of Danvers—Books 2-4
Kenrick, Hugh	Son of Garnet—Books 2-6
Kenrick, Sir Bowler	Ancestor—Book 2
Kenrick, Sir Stanier	Ancestor—Book 2
Knowlton, Samuel	Captain, Connecticut militia—Book 6
Lapworth, Mr.	Kidnapper—Book 1
Leggate, John	Actor/prop master—Book 1
LeGrand, Winslow	Dogmael Jones's secretary—Book 5
Leigh, Major Adam	Middlesex Brigade—Book 1
Leith, Isham	Innkeeper, murderer—Book 1
Lennox, Charles	3rd Duke of Richmond—Book 4
Levesque, Paul	Brother of Madeline McRae—Book 3
Lumley, Ideona	Play character—Book 1
Manners, William	Lieutenant, Captain Tallmadge's aide—Book 6
Marrable, Baron	Guest at Pumphrett concert—Book 2
Marriott, James	King's advocate, pamphleteer—Book 5
Marsh, Romney	A.K.A. Redmagne, as author of *Hyperborea*—Books 2-3
Massie, Capt. John	Planter, Morland Hall—Book 3
Maupin, Gabriel	Silversmith, cabinet maker—Books 3-5
McDougal, Alex	Scottish trader—Book 2
McDougal, Duncan	Father of Alex—Book 2
McLeod & McDougal	Scottish trading partnership—Book 3
McLeod, James	Partner of McDougal—Book 2
McRae, Etáin	Daughter of Ian—All Books
McRae, Ian	Father of Etáin, Scottish factor—Book 3
McRae, Madeline	Mother of Etáin—Books 1-3
Mendoza, Jacob	Pippin: Abraham/Alcyone—Book 2
Mercer, George	Burgess for Frederick, stamp distributor—Book 5
Meredith, William	MP for Liverpool—Books 4-5
Meservy, Robert	Pippin: Tobius/Tayete—Book 2
Milgram House	Dorset, Kenrick residence—Books 2-3
Moffet, Dorothy	Wife of James, Morland Hall—Books 3-4
Moffet, James	Tenant, Morland Hall—Books 3-4
Molyneux, Thomas	MP for Haslemere—Book 5

Montagu, John	4th Earl of Sandwich—Book 5
Morley, Millicent	Redmagne's mistress, Etáin's governess—Book 1
Mouse	Cooper, slave, Morland Hall—Book 3
Munford, Robert	Burgess, Mecklenburg, General Assembly—Book 4
Murray, John	Earl Dunmore, Governor of Virginia—Book 6
Murray, William	Baron Mansfield, Chief Justice, King's Bench—Books 4-5
Musto, Charles	Captain, *Charon*—Book 2
Nameless	MP for Bristol—Book 2
Nameless	MP for Craddock—Book 2
Nameless	MP for Norwich—Book 2
Nameless	MP for Nottingham—Book 2
Nameless	MP for Oxford—Book 2
Nameless	Junior Attorney-General—Book 2
Nameless	Junior Solicitor-General—Book 2
Nameless	Vicar of St. Brea's, Gwynnford—Book 1
Nameless	Sergeant, Sea Siren Tavern—Book 1
Nault, Henry	Warehouseman, Caxton—Book 5
Neaves, Mrs.	Wife of Spencer—Book 1
Neaves, Spencer	Merchant—Book 1
Nicholas, Robert C.	Burgess, York City, General Assembly—Books 4-6
Norris, Mr.	Easley's clerk—Book 3
North, Frederick "Lord"	MP for Banbury—Books 4-5
Nugent, Robert	MP for Bristol—Book 4
O'Such, Rory	A.K.A. Redmagne—Book 1
Ockhyser, John	Overseer, Meum Hall—Book 3
Olland, Will	Bosun, *Rainbow* Warship—Book 5
Onslow, Arthur	MP for Surrey, Speaker for Commons—Book 2
Ornsby, Lady	Guest at Pumphrett House—Book 2
Otway, Henry	Planter, Caxton—Books 3-4
Otway, Maura	Wife of Henry—Books 3-4
Otway, Morris	Son of Henry—Books 3-5
Oyston, Mr.	Kidnapper—Book 1
Paine, Thomas	Excise man, Lincolnshire—Book 4
Pannell, Sir Henoch	MP for Canovan, Revenue man—Books 1-6
Parmley, Robert	Pastor, Trelow—Book 1

Parrot, Sir James	King's Counsel, King's Bench, Pippin Trial—Books 3-5
Passmore, George	Tenant, Morland Hall—Books 3-4
Pendleton, Edmund	Burgess, Caroline County, General Assembly—Book 4
Petty, Agnes	Daughter of Mabel—Book 2
Petty, Mabel	Owner, Fruit Wench tavern, London—Book 2
Pitt, George	MP for Dorset—Book 5
Pitt, William	MP for Bath—Book 5
Plume, Chester	Skelly Gang—Book 1
Pompey	Slave, Meum Hall—Books 3-6
Pratt, Charles	Baron Camden, Chief Justice, Common Pleas—Book 5
Preeble, Mr.	Constable, Gwynnford—Book 1
Prescott, Col. Wm.	Massachusetts, Breed's Hill—Book 6
Primus	Slave/Overseer, Meum Hall—Book 3-4
Proudlocks, John	Tenant, Oneidan Indian, Morland Hall—Book 3-6
Pumphrett, Warren	Brother of Chloe—Books 1-2
Pumphrett-Pannell	(Chloe) Wife of Henoch—Books 2-4
Pursehouse, James	Kenrick banking partner—Book 3
Putnam, Israel	Brig. General, Massachusetts—Book 6
Rachel, Miss	Servant girl, Talbot household—Book 3
Ragsdale, Eyre	Major, commander of 6th Marine Battalion—Book 6
Ramsey, Michael	Ensign, Battle of Minden—Book 3
Ramshaw, John	Captain, *Sparrowhawk*—Books 1-5
Randolph, John	Chief Clerk, General Assembly—Book 4
Randolph, Peter	Governor's Council—General Assembly—Book 4
Randolph, Peyton	Attorney-General, Burgess, Williamsburg (brother of Peter and John, General Assembly)—Books 4-6
Redmagne	(Methuselah) A.K.A. Rory O'Such, et al.—Book 1
Reisdale, Thomas	Lawyer, Caxton—Books 3-5
Requardt, George	Captain, the *Busy*—Book 5
Rickerby, Nathan	Solicitor/landlord—Book 2
Rittles, Louise	Innkeeper, wife of Lucas—Book 3-4
Rittles, Lucas	Grocer, husband of Louise—Book 3-4
Rittles, Mr.	Hugh's tutor—Book 2
Roane, George	Under-sheriff, Caxton—Book 3-4
Robichaux, Paul	Captain, French privateer—Book 1

Robins, Obedience	Business agent, Morland Hall—Books 3-6
Robinson, John	Speaker, Burgess, King & Queen—Books 4-6
Robinson, William	Rev., Commissary of Virginia—Book 4
Rowland, Thomas	Captain, The *Busy*—Books 2-4
Rudge, Mr.	Gwynnford merchant—Book 1
Runcorn, Owen	Hugh's valet—Books 2-3
Russell, John	4th Duke of Bedford—Book 4
Sackville, Charles	MP for East Grimstead—Book 4
Sackville, George	MP for Hythe—Book 4
Safford, Steven	Proprietor, King's Arms Tavern, Caxton—Books 3-6
Sarah	Slave, Meum Hall—Book 3
Sargent, John	MP for West Looe—Book 5
Selwyn, James	Captain, 6th Marine Battalion—Book 6
Settle, William	Overlooker, Meum Hall—Book 3
Seymour, Henry	MP for Totnes—Book 5
Shakelady, Aubrey	Skelly Gang—Book 1
Shearl, Joseph	Carpenter, Meum Hall—Book 3
Shrubb, Richard	London alderman—Book 2
Skeats, Jubel	Sheriff, Gwynnford—Book 1
Skelly, Osbert	Augustus Magnus, gang leader, smuggler—Book 1
Smith, Champion	Slave—Book 3
Smith, John	A.K.A. Redmagne, original name—Book 1
Spears, Radulphus	Hugh's valet, Meum Hall—Books 3-6
Spranger, Mr.	Philadelphia merchant—Book 2
Stanhope, Philip D.	4th Earl of Chesterfield—Books 4-5
Stanley, Hans	MP for Southampton Borough—Book 5
Stannard, Arthur	British tobacco agent, Caxton—Books 3-5
Stannard, Joseph	Son of Arthur—Books 3-6
Stannard, Winifred	Wife of Arthur—Books 3-6
Stark, Col. John	New Hampshire regiments, Breed's Hill—Book 6
Sterling, Walter	Capt., *Rainbow*, Hampton Roads—Book 5
Stobb, Mr.	Constable, Danvers—Book 2
Stodwell, Mr.	Bookseller—Book 2
Sutherland & Bain	Scottish tobacco importers, McRae's firm—Books 3-6
Swain, Glorious	Pippin: Muir/Maia—Book 2

Swart, Amos	Planter, Brougham Hall—Book 3
Swart, Felise	Wife of Amos—Book 3
Sweeney, Daniel	Pippin: Claude/Celaeno—Book 2
Swire, John	Kenrick banking partner—Book 2
Talbot & Spicer	Merchants, Philadelphia—Books 2-4
Talbot, Otis	Merchant, Kenrick colonial agent—Books 2-5
Taller & Wyshe	Printers, London—Book 2
Tallmadge, Drew	Father of Roger—Books 2-3
Tallmadge, Francis	Brother of Roger—Book 2
Tallmadge, Roger	Hugh's friend, officer, MP for Bromhead—Books 2-6
Threap, Caleb	Tenant, Morland Hall—Books 3-4
Tippet, Cabal	Sheriff, Caxton—Books 2-6
Tippet, Muriel	Wife of Cabal—Books 3-6
Topham, Moses	Carpenter, Morland Hall—Books 2-6
Townshend, Charles	MP for Harwich, Board of Trade—Books 4-5
Townshend, Thomas	MP for Whitchurch—Book 4
Tragle, Buell	Master of seized *Sparrowhawk*—Book 6
Trantham, Drury	Hero of *Hyperborea*—All Books
Treverlyn, Fulke	Prosecutor, Falmouth trial, MP for Old Boothby—Books 1-5
Trigg, John	A.K.A. Redmagne/"London" alias—Book 1
Trist, Toby	Play character—Book 1
Trott, Agnes	Daughter of Hiram—Book 1
Trott, Hiram	Owner, Sea Siren tavern—Book 1
Trott, Jim	Son of Hiram—Book 1
Tuck, Elmo	Cook, Skelly Gang—Book 1
Tucker, John	Kenricks' coachman—Book 2
Turley, Jared	Bastard son of Earl (aka "Mr. Hunt")—Books 4-6
Twycross, Hugo	Justice—presiding judge, Falmouth trial—Book 1
Vere, Ann	Housekeeper, Meum Hall—Books 3-6
Vishonn, Annyce	Daughter of Reece, marries Morris Otway—Books 3-4
Vishonn, Barbara	Wife of Reece—Books 3-6
Vishonn, James	Son of Reece—Books 3-6
Vishonn, Reece	Planter, Caxton—Books 3-6
Walthoe, Nathaniel	Clerk of the Virginia Council—Book 5

Ward, Artemas	Commander, Breed's (Bunker) Hill—Book 6
Warren, Dr. Joseph	Massachusetts patriot—Book 6
Washington, George	Burgess, Frederick, General Assembly—Book 4
Weddle, Umphlett & Co.	London tobacco importers, Stannard's firm—Book 2
Westcott, Emery	Portrait painter—Books 2-4
Whately, Thomas	MP for Ludgershall, Grenville's secretary—Books 4-5
Wicker, James	Justice, Falmouth—Book 1
Wilbourne, Andrew	Viscount—Book 2
Wilkes, John	MP for Aylesbury—Books 4, 6
Wolfe, James	Lt. Colonel—Book 2
Worley, Benjamin	Proprietor, Worley & Sons—Books 2-6
Worley, Joseph	Son of Benjamin—Book 2
Worley, Lemuel	Son of Benjamin—Book 2
Worley, Mrs.	Wife of Benjamin—Book 2
Wynne, Rev.	Vicar of St. Quarrell's, Danvers—Book 2
Wythe, George	Burgess, Elizabeth City—Books 4-6
Zimmerman, Isaac	Tenant, Morland Hall—Books 3-6
Zouch, Henry	Brickmaster, Meum Hall—Books 3-6

MEUM HALL STAFF:

Business Agent:	Rupert Beecroft
Overlooker:	William Settle
Overseer:	John Ockhyser
Housekeeper:	Ann Vere
Cook:	Fiona Chance
Servant/Valet:	Radulphus Spears
Carpenter:	Joseph Shearl
Brickmaster	Henry Zouch
Slaves:	Bristol, Champion Smith, Cypriot,
	Cupid, Benabe, Jem, Bilico, Primus, Pompey
	Female: Sarah, Dilch, Diana, Rachel, Delia, Malkin

MORLAND STAFF:

Business Agent:	Obedience Robins
Overlooker:	William Hurry
Housekeeper:	Susannah Giddens
Cook:	Mary Beck
Servant:	Ruth Dakin
Carpenter:	Moses Topham
Coopers:	Mouse, Henry Dakin
Brickmaker:	Aymer Crompton
Tenants:	George Passmore, Isaac Zimmerman, James & Dorothy Moffet, Caleb Threap, Timothy Bigelow, John Proudlocks

SHIP NAME	TYPE
Amelia	Merchantman, sloop
Amherst	Merchant sloop, formerly the *Nancy*
Antares	Merchantman
Ariadne	Merchantman, schooner, the Kenricks' own vessel
Atlantic Conveyor	Merchantman
Basilisk	Customs sloop-of-war, 8 guns, 8 swivels, Turley's ship (formerly the *Nassau*)
Belfast	Merchant sloop
Busy	Merchantman, Worley & Sons, American trade
Charon	Merchantman
Cronus	East Indiaman
Diligence	Sloop-of-war, Chesapeake Bay, 12 guns, 12 swivels, 100 crew
Dolphin	Merchantman
Dorothea	Slave ship
Durand	French privateer
Excelsior	Merchant schooner
Friendly	Merchantman
Fowey	Frigate, 6th rate, 24 guns, 160 crew, sunk by shore batteries at Yorktown, 10/10/81

Galvin	Merchantman
George's Pleasure	Merchantman, sloop
Greyhound	Drury Trantham's ship (in *Hyperborea*)
Hare	Frigate (nicknamed the *Tortoise*)
Hasty Hart	Merchantman, Skelly's smuggling vessel
Helios	Warship, frigate, convoy
Jason	Warship, frigate, convoy
La Fleu	French privateer "The Scourge"
La Voleur	French privateer "The Thief"
Magdalen	Schooner (Royal Navy)
Manx	Slave ship, Royal African Company
Mercury	Frigate, 20 guns
Morag	Merchant schooner (Scottish)
Nassau	Seized by Hunt, renamed *Basilisk* (Turley's raider)
Nimble	Merchantman, Worley & Sons, European trade
Osprey	Merchantman
Otter	Warship
Pegasus	Merchantman, Skelly's—pre-outlaw years
Pericles	Merchantman
Peregrine	Merchantman
Prudence	Merchant brig owned by Novus Easley
Rainbow	Warship, 5th-rate frigate, Chesapeake Bay, 44 guns, 280 crew
Regale	East Indiaman
Regulas	Merchantman
Roilance	Merchantman
Rose	Warship, frigate
Rover	Warship, frigate
Skate	Merchant sloop
Sparrowhawk	Merchantman, Ramshaw's (later Geary's, then Hunt's)
Swiftsure	Merchantman, sloop
Tacitus	Merchantman, brig
Thunderer	Warship, line
William/Dunmore	Merchantman, seized by Dunmore for quarters
Zeus	Warship, frigate, convoy

THE POLITICAL
SPEECHES OF *SPARROWHAWK*

Compiled by Edward Cline

A key element in the character of the *Sparrowhawk* series—perhaps
even of its appeal to readers—is its political speeches. The principal
ones are included here, spoken in Parliament and the Virginia House of
Burgesses by Henoch Pannell, Colonel Isaac Barré, Dogmael Jones,
Hugh Kenrick, Patrick Henry, and William Pitt. Two of these speeches
are actual speeches, one by Barré, the other by Pitt. The others,
including Patrick Henry's Stamp Act Resolves speech, I wrote myself.
Henry's was composed around the fragments of that unrecorded speech
remembered by men years later. Barré is important because he was one
of the few British parliamentarians who understood the American
colonists; he warned his fellow legislators not to take the colonists or
their loyalty to the mother country for granted; his warning fell on deaf
ears. Pitt is important because, while he sided with the Americans, he
inadvertently handed Parliament and its career depredators an excuse to
continue to pursue policies intended to reduce Americans to servitude.

The best eighteenth–century political speakers, in the colonies and
in Britain, were trained in oratory and rhetoric. They could deliver
hours-long speeches without so much as a note, and make sense. Even
the villains of the time were adept in oratory, and it took a keen mind to
see through their sophistry. While I composed sermons, doggerels, the
occasional newspaper article, and even sketched two political cartoons

for the series, I derived special pleasure in writing the speeches. Early on I realized that if one were going to recreate the British-American culture and politics of the period, political speeches must form an integral part of the epic. If men were moved passionately by the ideas of freedom—or dead set against them—how better to dramatize the passion and the opposition than by showing what was thought and said?

To read these extemporaneous speeches, one cannot help but note an essential difference between them and what passes for oratory today. Most modern politicians cannot speak two complete sentences together from memory without the aid of a written text, extensive notes, or a teleprompter. Most of them do not—in fact, cannot—write their own speeches, but rely on hired speechwriters, whose efforts doubtless are endlessly rewritten to conform to what a speaker wishes his auditors to believe he is saying or what he thinks they wish to hear. Further, their speeches are largely ragouts of "messages"; that is, of unappetizing stews of refried bromides, lubricious principles, and populist claptrap, all calculated to appeal to men's emotions, not to their minds. Modern speechmaking is a monument to vapidity. I cannot recall the last time I heard a living American politician declaim on individual rights, freedom of speech, or the sanctity of private property.

So, it was with great relief and pleasure that I could retreat to a time when these matters were a common subject of speechmaking.

* * *

Sir Henoch Pannell, member for Canovan, and dedicated enemy of the American colonies, gives his maiden speech in Parliament, 1755.

"It has been heard in this assembly on a number of occasions that the colonials are unhappy with the means with which this coming war is to be paid for and prosecuted. Oh, how they grumble, those rustical Harries! The means, as we all know, and as they rightly fear, must in the end come out of their own rough, bucolic purses. To my mind, that is but a logical expectation. Yet, you would think, to judge by some of the protestations that have reached our ears, that the Crown was proposing to engage the French over Madagascar for possession of that pirates' nest, and obliging them to pay the costs of an adventure far removed from their concerns. But—the threat is to their own lives, their own homes and families, their fields, their shops, their seaports, their own livelihoods, and they higgle and haggle over the burden of expense! A very *strange* state of mind, indeed! I am merely a messenger, sirs. Do not entertain thoughts of murdering me for what I have said, or am about to say.

"And, no doubt, many of these same said colonials will pay with their own skins, too. However, if the reports of officers in His Majesty's service in the colonies in the past are to be warranted—and I don't for a minute doubt the substance of their complaints or the truth of their anecdotes—not many colonial skins will be cut by French bayonet or bruised by Indian war club. The colonials, it is commonly said, are uniformly lazy, undisciplined, contentious, quarrelsome, niggardly, presumptuous, and cowardly, amongst themselves as well as amongst our brave officers and troops! It is thought by many in high and middling places that if the colonial auxiliaries under General Braddock's command had been more forthright and daring with their musketry in that fatal wood near the Ohio, that brave and enterprising officer would be sitting in this very chamber today to receive our thanks, and not buried in some ignominious patch of mud in the wilderness. But—the colonial temperament is a matter of record. *Our* colonials! Scullions all, the sons of convicts, whores, and malcontents! From the greedy gentry of the northern parts, to the posturing macaronis of the southern, every man Jack of them unmindful of the fact that he is a *colonial*, a mere plant nurtured in exotic soil for the benefit of this nation! Oh! How *ungrateful*, our Britannic flora!

"Yes! *Ungrateful*, their noggins emboldened by a few leagues of water! Now, it is thought here in this hall, and in London, and in all of England, and even in Wales and Scotland, that His Majesty's government—we here, within these ancient walls, and *they* across the way, in *Lords* are the corporate lawgiver *and* defender of our excellent constitution. Why, the most ignoble knife-grinder and blasphemous fishwife would be able to tell you that! Yet, proposals for new laws, or for the repeal of old ones, or for changes in existing statutes from colonial legislatures—those self-important congresses of coggers, costermongers, and cork farmers—arrive by the bulging barrelful on nearly every merchant vessel that drops anchor at Custom House. These proposals are dutifully conveyed by liveried but sweaty porters to the Privy Council and the Board of Trade, to the Admiralty and the Surveyor-General and the Commissioner of Customs.

"I am not friend to many members of those august bodies, but they truly have my sympathies, for they have the thankless task of sorting through those mountains of malign missives to segregate the specious from the serious. Many of these pleadings and addresses are shot through with a constant harping on the rights of the colonials as Englishmen, and so on with that kind of blather, like a one-tune hurdy-gurdy, a tiresome thing to endure, as many of you can attest. Virginia and Massachusetts are particularly monotonous and noisome in this respect. The planters would like to sell their weed directly to Spain or Holland, without the benefit of our lawful brokerage, while the Boston felt factors wish to fashion their own hats for sale there—or *here*!—without the material ever crossing the sea to be knocked together by our own artists. Well, sirs! We must needs remind our distant brethren that we are busy bees, too, and that the rights of Englishmen are only as good as the laws we enact allow—*here*, as well as *there*!

"Gentlemen, must I ask these questions? Does the beadle instruct the university? Does the postilion choose his employer's destination? Does the bailiff counsel the magistrate? *No!* Should the colonials be permitted to advise *us* of *our* business? No! This is a custom unwisely indulged and which must be corrected! They must be reminded as civilly but as strenuously as possible that they are residents of that far land at this nation's leisure, pleasure, expense, and tolerance! This nation's, *and* His Majesty's! They wish us to respect their rights. Well, and why not? We would not deny them those rights. But, if they wish a greater role in the public affairs of this empire, let them repatriate themselves to this fair island, and queue up at the polling places—*here!*—where they may exercise those *native* rights on the soil from which they and those rights have sprung!

"Yes! For that is the nub of the matter! *Here* they will find no special circumstances, no calculated abridgement of their rights! *There* in New York, and in Boston, in Philadelphia, and Williamsburg, and Charleston, they find themselves in special circumstances that necessitate abridgement, and like it not! But—they elect to be *there*, and not *here*! And if they cannot purchase this simple reasoning, if they persist in pelting us with petitions, memorials, and remonstrances, *I* say it must be the time to forget civility, and chastise the colonials as good parents would wisely chastise wayward and misbehaved children!"

Pannell is interrupted at this point by another member of the House who questions what relevance his ranting has to the question of how to finance the new war with France.

"You are so right, sir! Will the House please forgive me my enthusiasm, my passion, and my misfired patriotism? I leave the floor so that the debate on the particulars of finance may continue."

* * *

SPEECHES FOR AND AGAINST THE STAMP ACT
PARLIAMENT, FEBRUARY 1765

Colonel Isaac Barré, member for Chipping Wycombe, replied with indignation to another member's speech about the ingratitude of the colonials.

"They planted by *your* care? No! Your oppressions planted them in America! They fled from *your* tyranny to a then uncultivated and inhospitable country...They nourished by *your* indulgence? They grew up by *your* neglect of them! And as soon as you began to care about them, that care was exercised in sending persons to rule over them, sent to spy out their liberty, to misrepresent their actions and to prey upon them, men whose behavior on many occasions has caused the blood of those sons of liberty to recoil within them!...They protected by *your* arms? They have nobly taken up arms in your defense, have exerted a valor amidst their constant and laborious industry for the defense of a country whose frontier and interior parts have yielded all its little savings to your emolument...Remember I this day told you so, that spirit of freedom which actuated that people at first will accompany them still...However superior to me in general knowledge and experience the reputable body of this House may be, yet I claim to know more of America than most of you, having seen and been conversant in that country. The people I believe are as truly loyal as any subjects the king has, but a people jealous of their liberties and who will vindicate them if ever they should be violated..."

Sir Dogmael Jones, member for Swansditch and an ally of Hugh Kenrick, also speaks against Prime Minister George Grenville's proposed Stamp Act. He rises after Colonel Barré.

"I commend my valued colleague, the member for Chipping Wycombe, for his brave and heart-felt words. They will be remembered, when my own and others' are not.

"The maxim with which the honorable minister [*Grenville*] concluded his address may have been appropriate and enough for our ancestors, in a distant time when kings were true kings, barons true barons, commoners the dross and drudge of the realm, and when all were ignorant of a larger canvas of things. In point of fact, that maxim applied exclusively to kings and barons; commoners were never a party to its formulation, limited as they were by law and custom to merely support and obedience, a lesson harshly taught them on numerous occasions.

"But much progress has been made since those ancient and brutal times, and things seen but dimly then are clearly perceived in these. It is neither appropriate nor enough for us to pursue a policy or pass an act founded on that maxim; to attempt it would be a call for a return to dullness and ignorance. After all, the man whose genius ended our dependency on that maxim was Mr. John Locke, and I very much doubt that any of us here today could credibly dispute him in the most carefully prepared disquisition. And while this nation may have so corrupted and compromised his clarity on the issue of rights versus power—or perhaps even repudiated it—we all here today should be mindful that the colonials—those 'sons of liberty,' as they were just now so trenchantly knighted by my esteemed colleague—the colonials take Mr. Locke very seriously. The conflict which the honorable minister labored at the beginning to deny exists, is not so much a political one, as a philosophic one, and I feel it my duty to inform the honorable minister and his party that *Nature* is, and will continue to be, on the side of the Americans.

"Nature will rise up and either overturn a corrupt system, or abandon it in a vindication of natural right.

"I had planned, on the opportunity to speak, to review the honorable minister's record as evidence of his hostility to British liberty, by citing, among so many instances, his purchase of the Isle of Man in order to extinguish the smuggling trade there—a trade born and sustained under the aegis of taxation—his efforts to more efficiently collect land and salt taxes, his frustrated attempts to conquer Jersey and Guernsey, and most especially his campaign against publishers and printers in this very metropolis who evade the same stamp tax.

"But his address was evidence enough of that hostility. The purpose of his proposed tax, he says, is to help defray the costs of maintaining an army in North America and a navy in its waters. Consequently, that part of the Crown budget would be reserved for its usual outlays. The budget, of course, rests on revenues, and those are derived from taxes. And for what purpose are all those taxes laid and collected in an ever-mounting debt? Why, to sustain an overbearing, conceited stratum of placeholders, receivers of pensions, and beneficiaries of perpetual gratuities. It is for their sake that these laws and taxes are enacted and enforced—and subsequently flouted and evaded. So much money is diverted to sustain so much *nothing*, when it could go to increasing the tangible prosperity of this nation under the shield of genuine liberty, which I hasten to stress is not to be confused with the shallow, corrupted, mockish husk of it that we boast of now. We should blush in contrition when we are complimented by men abroad, and even compliment ourselves, for that vaunted liberty.

"The establishment of the sustained and the entitled do not object to prosperity, and they have a mean, grudging regard for liberty, so long as the prosperity guarantees their causeless incomes, so long as liberty does not impinge upon or threaten to deprive them of their lucre. I ask this question, not queried by the honorable minister: Can we expect the colonials to grow in prosperity under the insidious burden he proposes to lay upon them, and can the obdurate stratum of the idle expect to profit from their certain poverty?

"I ask this House—or that half of it who deign to attend today—not to rush to oblige the honorable minister until they have devoted some hard thought to this tax. I invite the proponents of these resolutions to set aside some time to ponder the contradictions inherent in their policies, actions, and desires. I likewise invite my colleagues in opposition to consider the folly of their concessions to the honorable minister's principal arguments. If his administration derives any strength at all on this matter, it comes not from his party, but from the fatal confusion of the well-meaning of *our* party, one not dissimilar from that of a thirsty, shipwrecked man who, out of desperation, drinks sea water for want of a purer, uncontaminated elixir.

"I end here with my own warning, sirs. I do not expect the Americans—for let us refer to the colonials as Americans, and not mistake them, as the honorable minister will not, for Englishmen—I do not expect them to submit to this tax except at the prodding of a bayonet or legislative extortion, and, perhaps, not even then. If you contrive to humble them, you should not expect that they shall long remain in the thralldom of humility, for perhaps we are all mistaken, and they are not Englishmen at all, but the inhabitants of another kingdom.

"Colonel Barré is correct when he warns that the Americans will not surrender their birthright—and I refer to that expounded by Mr. Locke—for a mess of pottage, no matter how much you dulcify the bowl with bounties, rate reductions, and similar bribes for them to remain on their knees. I am confident they will tire of the business and assert their full freedom.

"In conclusion, I am grateful that a man of subtler persuasion is not at the helm of this matter, for that man may at least depend on the esteem in which the Americans hold him, and thus be able to persuade them to concede and capitulate. But we all know that he would possess the wisdom not to pursue the folly."

Sir Henoch Pannell, now a political enemy of Dogmael Jones, rises in answer to Barré and Jones:

"I had not planned to speak today, sirs, but late, offensive words make it my duty to. I commend the honorable minister on so clear a presentation of his bill. I will say at the beginning that I may be relied upon to support his resolutions now before this committee to be discussed, and any amendments to them in future, for such are surely to occur in this contentious House. And, I oppose Sir William's motion to postpone a vote on the resolutions. They are a simple, uncomplex matter to be simply disposed of.

"I will say further that the honorable minister's scheme is an ingenious one that will relieve this nation of some of the expense of victory, by obliging our colonies to contribute their equitable—and, may I say, *tardy*—share of that expense, for, as the honorable minister so aptly pointed out, the greatest part of that expense went to the preservation of those colonies, and of their liberties. In brief, I concur with every reason and sentiment offered by the honorable minister that this should be so—but for one or two trifling ones.

"The honorable minister contends that if the colonials were not subject to this proposed tax, 'they are not entitled to the privileges of Englishmen.' With all modesty, and with the greatest deference to his experience, and only seeming to agree with the member for Swansditch, may I point out to the House an error in cogitation here? *I* say that the colonials have *never* been Englishmen, for they have *never* been burdened by the proposed tax, which, it is a matter of common knowledge, is simply an extension of the one we pay there, and have paid since the time of Charles the Second. That fact constitutes an onerous kind of *privilege*. And, on that point, I will carry the honorable minister's assertion one step further, and contend that if they wish to be Englishmen, let the colonials submit to this and other taxes, and praise this body and His Majesty for the opportunity. It is *they* who have been negligently privileged all these decades. It is time for them to earn the glorious appellation of Englishmen.

"Allow me, patient sirs, to point out not so much as another error in the honorable minister's assumptions, as an oversight. As I do not regard the colonials—and I mean those on the continent, I do not include our West Indian colleagues here today— as I do not regard those persons as true Englishmen, I say that the colonies ought *not* to be represented in this House, and for two reasons.

"The first is that historians of my acquaintance record that the colonies of ancient Greece and Rome were not represented in the legislatures of their capitals. They were *administered*, not represented! At times wisely, at other times, not so. That is beside the point. I do not believe that any colonial has been so foolish as to request representation, nor do I believe that the honorable minister has seriously contemplated the notion even in the abstract. Still, the question to ask is: Why should we make precedent and depart from that policy?

"The second reason I must broach at the risk of confounding my first. I wish to offer my shoulder with others in the sad but necessary duty of pallbearer in the funeral of the colonial complaint of taxation without representation in this House. The colonies *are* represented—as the honorable minister explained—even though their populations are not even counted among the one-tenth or one-twentieth of the enfranchised populace of this nation who are directly represented. That is the way the Constitution and custom have arranged matters, and that is that. Now, we hear no similar complaints of non-representation from those towns and regions of this isle that do not send members here. That is because those people *know* they are represented, in spirit, in the abstract, in kind—*virtually*, as that oft-heard word describes their situation. And, they submit with happiness to Parliament's authority.

"The colonies, however, exist by grace of the Crown and His Majesty and for the benefit of this nation, and I have always questioned the folly of allowing them the leave to determine expenditures and their own methods of allocation and collection. The colonies have of late been especially hard-mouthed over the reins of supervision from this House and the Board of Trade. They have not been properly *lunged*, sirs, and they will never be ridden unless a commanding hand takes them under training.

"I believe I made a speech on this vexatious colonial matter some time ago—why, at the beginning of the late war! I believe I warned this House, then sitting in a Committee of Supply, that this colonial pestering and posturing over the twin mooncalves of taxation and representation would not abate, would not cease until Parliament scolded its children and banished all discussion of the matter. My remarks were dismissed then, not without good cause, for I had, in the heat of my concerns, digressed from the business then before the committee. I will not belabor the points I made then, but only repeat that if these colonials wish to be represented, let them come *here* and take up residence, so that they may be properly represented! Some of them have done so. There is Mr. Huske, born and reared in New Hampshire. And there is Mr. Abercromby, who, although born here, spent so much time in the southern plantations, that he acquired a unique but not unpleasant pattern of speech. Now, they are not only represented—they represent!

"Have patience with my support, sirs. I come to a close here. Having been curious about the origins of the word that has given us so much pother, I availed myself of the wisdom of some notable wordsmiths—etymologists, I believe they are called—and my consultations allowed me to discover that two possible meanings may be had from the word *colony*. Friends of the resolutions may adopt either meaning with no prejudice to their good sense and regard for truth. The first meaning is indeed ancient, for our word *colony*, coming down to us from the Romans and Greeks without loss of implication, means to *coloniate* with husbandmen and tenants on a property. And, indeed, what are our own colonists, or colonials, but husbandmen and tenants of His Majesty's estates? They must be that, or why do we impose quitrents on them? Keep that fact in mind, sirs, when you think upon the justice of the honorable minister's proposed tax.

"The other meaning can be taken to suggest—and the House will please forgive the indelicate but necessary reference, for there is no other way to talk of it—the route of egress of the *bile* and *waste* of the kingdom, with which these same estates have been notoriously populated and *manured* for so many years. Of course, sirs, I appropriate the first meaning in strictest decorum, while I leave the second to be caricatured in private conversation for deserved levity.

"Well, sirs, that is the gist of my thoughts. Mr. Townshend there made relevant reference to the ingratitude of distempered children and the grief they bring to their parents. *Our* colonial children are wayward and profligate, and it is time that they were bled so that they may be cured of their outlandish distemper. The honorable minister's tax can but only cure them of it, and then this kingdom and its colonies will again be a happy family."

* * *

SPEECHES AGAINST THE STAMP ACT
The Virginia House of Burgesses, 29-30 May 1765

Hugh Kenrick's Stamp Act Speeches, the first spoken to prepare the House for the introduction of Patrick Henry's Resolves, the second spoken after they have been introduced and open to debate.

"Sirs, a man's powers of persuasion rest not solely in his eloquence, but in how successful his style orders the facts he presents. I ask you, therefore, not to judge my eloquence, but the facts.

"Let us proceed to those facts, and scan some simple arithmetic. It is claimed by the authors and proponents of the Stamp Act, a copy of which is now in the custody of this House, that from these colonies, the levies enumerated in that act will raise some one hundred thousand pounds per annum. It is not denied by these gentlemen that the tax is an internal one, nor that it has been one long in contemplation. They make no distinction between that tax, taxes on our exports and imports, and any passed by this or any other colonial assembly. Nor should we, but that is another matter to be taken up, in future. We are assured by these gentlemen, the authors of this act, that the revenue raised by this new tax—a tax that may be paid in sterling *only*, let me stress that aspect, neither in kind nor in our own notes, but in rare sterling—that the revenue will remain in the colonies to defray the cost of the army here.

"Well, sirs, here is an instance of Punic faith! Britain may rightly abhor a standing army. Britain, so close to her regular enemies France, Spain, and the Netherlands, can exist in security and confidence without the burden and imposition of a standing army! We colonies, however, are spared that abhorrence, even though our close enemies to the west are less a threat to us than a single French privateer! Why are we to be relieved of that just fear? Well, you have all read the Proclamation of two years past. Allow me to read to you the reasons behind that qualification, that ominous exception, written by eminences in London who lay claim to being *friends* of these colonies.

"Here is what a person in the train of Lord Shelburne wrote in his recommendations of policy: 'The provinces now being surrounded by an army, a navy, and by hostile tribes of Indians, it may be time, not to oppress or injure them, but to exact a *due deference* to the just and equitable demands of a British Parliament.' And, here is what an agent for Georgia wrote in recommendation: 'Troops and fortifications will be very necessary for Great Britain to keep up in her colonies, if she intends to settle their dependency on her.'

"It is such recommendations that influenced the wording and intent of the Proclamation, sirs. I trust I needn't repeat the encircling particulars of that document. The records of the Board of Trade, of the Privy Council, of the Secretary of State, are rife with such recommendations, written, for the most part, by subministers and under–secretaries.

"What is the estimated cost of our standing army? Mr. Grenville asserts four hundred thousand pounds per annum. Where will the balance of that estimate come from, other than from the projected one hundred thousand raised by this stamp? In the best conjecture, from here, from there, but mostly from *us*, by way of all the duties we pay on manufactures and necessities brought into these colonies. Parliamentary trade estimates show that these colonies provide the Crown with a revenue of two millions per annum. That number represents not only our purchases, but all duties, indirect excises, and other charges and levies paid by us. What assurances have we that neither the army nor its subsidy here will not grow? *None.*

"More arithmetic, sirs. Not all of you have had the opportunity to peruse the tome of taxation now resting on the Clerk's table. I now read to you some of the new costs to you and your fellow Virginians, when this statute becomes active law—when the trigger is pressed on November first." *(Here, Hugh reads many of the stamp duties for the House.)*

"Paltry sums, to be sure, you may be thinking—paltry to His Majesty, who thinks nothing of spending one hundred thousand pounds to guarantee his party's election to the Commons, or to purchase a party there after an election. Paltry sums, sirs, but are *we* so prosperous and solvent that we can pay them? If the Crown will not accept our notes, even after discounting, or Spanish or French silver, with what can we pay these duties? With our credit? We have all but exhausted our credit with the mother country and the merchants there. If new credit is to be granted us, on what terms?

"So much for the arithmetic, gentlemen. On to the *budget* of our liberty, and to what lays ahead for us if we submit *humbly* to the authority of this statute.

"Firstly, we will have conceded to Parliament the right and power to levy this tax, a tax contrived and imposed in careless violation of precedent, legality, and our liberties. This tax, sirs, if admitted and tolerated by us, will surely serve as an overture to other taxes and other powers. And, having granted Parliament that power *in absentia*—a power to raise a revenue from us, which was never the object of any of the navigation and commercial laws, burdensome and arbitrary in themselves—we will also have invited Parliament to render *this* body, and all colonial legislatures, redundant and superfluous! What would be the consequence of that negligence? That we would have representation neither here nor in Parliament! The very purpose and function of this assembly will have been obviated! This chamber, though occupied by men, would become a shell, a mockery! Think ahead, gentlemen. What would then prevent Parliament or the Board of Trade or the Privy Council from concluding that a costly assembly of voiceless and powerless burgesses should be forever dissolved? What would prevent the sages of Westminster from replacing a governor with a *lord-lieutenant*?

"Ah, sirs! Here is more arrogance in the offing! A *lord-lieutenant*, he says. What impudence! Impossible! Our charters grant us the right to governors, dependent on our assemblies for their pay! Well, sirs, there is talk in the dank closets of Westminster of revising the charters of all the colonies, in order to exact a 'due deference' from them! A lord-lieutenant, may I remind you gentlemen, has neither an assembly to address, nor one to answer to. Such a false 'governor' would not be dependent on the benefices of an elected assembly, but would be paid directly by the Crown from our stamped pockets and purses, to ensure enforcement of Crown law.

"And, here is another ominous provision of this Stamp Act, sirs. In any case concerning violation of it, a prosecutor may choose between the venues of a jury court, and a juryless admiralty court in which to try a defendant. I leave to your imaginations, sirs, to think of which court would regularly find defendants so charged at fault, and promote the careers of interested informants and Crown officers.

"What would we be left with, sirs? Nothing that we had ever prided ourselves in. We would become captives of the Crown, paying, toiling captives in a vast Bridewell prison! The one thing will follow the other, as surely as innocuous streams feed great rivers. Mr. Grenville is first minister now. Who will follow him? Another minister with his own notion of 'due deference'? I shall paraphrase something I heard uttered not long ago. It should matter little to us whether this law and the Proclamation are a consequence of premeditated policy, or of divers coincidences, when the same logical end is our *slavery*.

"'*Traitor*,' did you say, sir? Allow me to read to you the words of another 'traitor,' words on which I had planned to end my remarks, but which ought to shame you for having pronounced your one. 'The people who are the descendents of those, who were forced to submit to the yoke of a government by constraint, have always the right to shake it off, and free themselves from the usurpation, or tyranny, which the sword hath brought in upon them, till their rulers put them under such a frame of government, as they willingly, and of choice consent to.'

"That, sir, was Mr. John Locke, to whom we all owe a debt of thanks, and you, sir, an apology. I do not perceive in this Stamp Act, sirs, either our will, our choice, or our consent!

"The time to say 'No,' gentlemen, is *now*, and to give ambitious, careless men notice that we will not be ruled and bled to feebleness. If we succeed in a new, more vigorous protest, then the stage will be set for us to correct other imbalances, other injustices, other impositions. Better men than those who authored and passed this act are in Parliament now. They spoke for us. They were overwhelmed by the inertia of ignorance and the arrogance of avarice. But, if we stand our ground now, more like them will take heart and come to the fore, men who see in this encroachment jeopardy of liberty in England itself, men who recognize the possibility of a partnership between England and this ad hoc confederation of colonies. We are Britons, sirs, and will not be slaves! We are Virginians, sirs, and should be wise and proud enough to find this tax repugnant to the cores of our souls!

"Let us be known for our *Attic* faith!"

The next day, in defense of Patrick Henry's Resolves, and in answer to Attorney-General Peyton Randolph's remarks, Hugh rises to speak again:

"We who endorse these resolves are neither ignorant of the difference between foolishness and wisdom, nor oblivious to the virtues of those who have trod the earth before many of us came into it. Virtue, said Socrates, springs not from possessions—and

I mean here not merely our tangible wealth, but our liberties as well—not from possessions, but from virtue springs those possessions, and all other human blessings, whether for the individual or society. In these circumstances, the virtue which that gentleman accuses us of lacking, has become a vice. Call it moderation, or charity, it will not serve us now. We exercise the virtue of righteous certitude, for it alone has the efficacy that conciliation and accommodation have not. That virtue is expressed—and I believe that the honorable Colonel Bland there will concur with me on this point—that virtue is expressed in one of the original charters of this colony, and in the first charter of Massachusetts, and has merely been reiterated in these resolves, but in clearer language. Moral certitude is a virtue itself, and in this instance is a glorious one, because it asserts and affirms, in all those charters and resolves, our natural liberty and the blessings it bestows upon us!

"Let us not imbibe the hemlock of humility, duty, or deference, sirs! Socrates did not have a choice in that regard. *We* have. Should we choose to rest on the virtue boasted of and advocated by that more experienced gentleman, that will be a more certain path to the despair, defeat, and regret he fears, and we will have nothing left that we can call our own!"

* * *

PATRICK HENRY'S STAMP ACT SPEECH
29 May 1765

"I wish to introduce a number of resolutions to the committee for its sagacious consideration.

"Sirs, this House's original entreaties to Parliament and His Majesty in protest of the then contemplated Stamp Act—entreaties written in astonishing deference, but doubtless from a sense of reason and justice—stand as of this day without the reciprocate courtesy of reply, except in the enactment of this

Act. We therefore find ourselves in a predicament which will not correct itself, not unless we take corrective actions. Many members of this House are in agreement that stronger and clearer positions must be transmitted to those parties, in order to elicit from them a concern for this matter commensurate with our own, lest Parliament and His Majesty construe our silence for passive concession and submission.

"We propose that this House adopt and forward to those parties, not genuflective beseechments or adulatory objurgations, but pungent *resolves* of our understanding of the origins and practice of British and American liberty, resolves which will frankly alert them to both the error of their presumptions and our determination to preserve that liberty. These resolves, in order to have some consequence and value, ought not to be expressed by us in the role of effusive mendicants applying for the restitution of what has been wrested from them, but with the cogently blunt mettle of men who refuse to be robbed.

"And, what is it we are being robbed of? The recognized and eviternal right to govern ourselves without Parliamentary interference, meddling, supervision, or usurpation! As another member here has so well explained, the Stamp Act represents not merely the levying of taxes on our goods, but on our *actions* to preserve our property and livelihoods. This law, he explained, will serve to remove from the realm of most of the freemen in this colony, and in our sister colonies, all moral recourse to justice and liberty.

"Surely, some here will counter: *That* is not the intent of this law and those duties. But, nevertheless, wisdom prescribes *that consequence*. And, in the abstract, even should every man in this colony have the miraculous means to pay these duties, the question would remain: Ought they? For if submission is an imperative, then they ought to submit as well to laws that would assign them their diets, arrange their marriages, and regulate their amusements and diversions.

"I am certain that in the vast woodwork of British government, there lurks an army of interlopers and harpies whose notions of 'due deference' and an ordered, dutiful, captive society fancy that direction in the matter of governing these colonies, an army that, until now, has been kept in check by its fear of ridicule and by the regular, bracing tonic of reason. The Stamp Act alone will not prompt that army to forget its proper inhibitions. But, our submission to it will, and invite it to emerge from that worm-eaten woodwork like locusts to further infest our lives by leave of a Parliamentary prerogative that we failed to challenge.

"Challenges, sirs, not remonstrances, are in order today! Resolutions, not memorials!

"Look around you, gentlemen. This is *our* forum, *our* legislature. It is a living, honorable thing, this hall, because we may meet in it to conduct our own business. But, neglect to challenge this law, and I foresee the day when this hall of liberty will become a mausoleum, redolent with the fading echoes of a distant, glorious freedom which from shame you may be reluctant to remember, and of which your children will have no notion, because we failed. Posterity will not look kindly upon us, should we fail. What might happen to this chamber? Well, in one of the many inglorious chapters that comprise the downfall of ancient Rome, it is noted that the Hall of Liberty was made to serve as a barracks for the mercenaries of an emperor. But, perhaps events will be merciful, and this place will be burned and leveled by our wardens to prevent us from ever again presuming to conduct our own business without fear of offense or penalty.

"Here are some resolves.

"Whereas, the honorable House of Commons in England have of late drawn into question how far the General Assembly of this colony hath the power to enact laws for laying of taxes and imposing duties payable by the people of this, His Majesty's most ancient colony; for setting and ascertaining the same to all future times, the House of Burgesses of this present General Assembly have come to the following resolves.

"Resolved, that the first adventurers and settlers of this His Majesty's colony and dominion of Virginia brought with them, and transmitted to their posterity, and all other of His Majesty's subjects since inhabiting in this His Majesty's said colony, all the privileges and immunities that have at any time been held, enjoyed, and possessed by the people of Great Britain.

"Resolved, that by two royal charters, granted by King James the First, the colonists aforesaid are declared entitled to all the privileges, liberties, and immunities of denizens and natural-born subjects, to all intents and purposes, as if they had been abiding and born within the realm of England.

"Resolved, that the taxation of the people by themselves, or by persons chosen by themselves to represent them, who can only know what taxes the people are able to bear, and the easiest mode of raising them, and who must themselves be equally affected by such taxes—an arrangement," interjected Henry, "which is the surest security against burdensome taxation by our own representatives"—then continued to read from the page, "is the distinguishing characteristic of British freedom, and without which, the ancient Constitution cannot subsist.

"Resolve the fourth, gentlemen: That His Majesty's liege people of this his most ancient and loyal colony of Virginia, have without interruption enjoyed the precious right of being thus governed *by their own Assembly* in the article of their taxes and internal police, and that the same hath *never* been forfeited or in any other way given up or surrendered, but hath been constantly recognized by the kings and people of Great Britain.

"Those, sirs, are the premises of a uniquely extended syllogism. Here is its conclusion.

"Resolved, that the General Assembly of this colony have the *only* and *sole* exclusive right and power to lay taxes and impositions upon the inhabitants of this colony, and that every attempt to vest such power in any person or persons whatsoever, other than the General Assembly of this colony, has a manifest tendency to destroy British as well as American freedom!

"There are two more resolves to be read, sirs, but these five are their foundation, and must be adopted before the sixth and seventh can have any meaning or force."

The next day, in reply to criticisms of the "violence" of the Resolves, Henry answers:

"If *this* House elects to wait on Parliament, sirs, may I ask in what capacity? Ought we to wait idle in the foyer of those eminences' concerns, in the mental livery of a menial, while they complete the latest business of oppressing the good people of England, not daring to whisper the persecution of their own brethren, lest it some how insinuate our own? Some men in this chamber may prefer to approach the bar of Parliament, hats in hand, on raw knees, as humble supplicants, in search of redress and restitution. *I*, sirs, prefer to wait for Parliament to call on *me*, to beg *my* forgiveness for that body's attempt to dupe and enslave me *and* this my country!"

Given a second chance to speak, Henry rises and verbally accosts the Attorney-General, Peyton Randolph, who had delivered a speech advocating conciliation.

"The honorable gentleman there spoke now, not of the rightness or wrongness of the resolve in question, but of ominous consequences, should this House adopt it. I own that I am perplexed by his attention to what the Crown can and may do, and by his neglect to speak to the propriety of the resolve and the impropriety of this Stamp Act. Should he have examined for us the basis of his fears? Yes. But, he did not. Perhaps he concluded that they were too terrible to articulate. So, *I* shall examine them, for I believe that he and I share one well-founded fear: The power of the Crown to punish us, to scatter us, to despoil us, for the temerity of asserting in no ambiguous terms *our* liberty! *I* fear that power no less than he. But, I say that such a fear, of such a power, can move a man to one of two courses. He can make a compact with that power, one of mutual *accommodation*, so that he may live the balance of his years in the shadow of that power, ever-trembling in soul-dulling funk lest that power rob him once again.

"Or—he can rise up, and to that power say '*No!*', to that power proclaim: 'Liberty cannot, and will not, ever accommodate tyranny! I am wise to that Faustian bargain, and will not barter piecemeal or in whole *my* liberty!'

"Why are you gentlemen so fearful of that word? Why have not one of you dared pronounce it? Is it because you believe that if it is not spoken, or its fact or action in any form not acknowledged, it will not be what it is? Well, *I* will speak it for you and for all this colony to hear!

"*Tyranny! Tyranny! Tyranny!* There! The horror is named *Tyranny!* There is its guise, sirs! What a Janus-faced object it is, smirking at you on one side of its mask, shedding tears for you on the other! What a contemptible set of men who authored it, but whom you wish to *accommodate*! What a disgraceful proposition! And what a travesty you ask us to condone! 'Tis only a mere pound of flesh we propose to remove from you, they tell you in gentle, proper language, and we promise that you will not bleed. *Hah!* You will recall how the Bard proved the folly and fallacy of that kind of compact! Are not accommodation and compromise another but greater form of it? He proved it in a comedy, sirs! You propose to prove it in a tragedy, and if you succeed in penning *finis* to your opus, *you* may rue the day you put your names on its title page!

"You gentlemen, you have amassed vast, stately libraries from which you seem to be reluctant to cull or retain much wisdom. Know that I, too, have books, and that they are loose and dog-eared from my having read them, and I have profited from that habit.

"History is rife with instances of ambitious, grasping tyranny! Like many of you, I, too, have read that in the past, the tyrants Tarquin and Julius Caesar each had his Brutus, Catiline had his Cicero and Cato, and, closer to our time, Charles had his Cromwell! George the Third may—"

It is here that many burgesses rose and accused Henry with speaking treason.

"—may George the Third profit by their example!...If this be treason, then make the most of it!"

* * *

SPEECHES FOR REPEAL OF THE STAMP ACT
Parliament, March 1766

William Pitt, member for Bath in the Commons, but virtual Prime Minister over Rockingham (Pitt would form his own government the same year, and also be elevated to Lords, a move meant to diminish his political influence), spoke for repeal of the Stamp Act, but in terms that left open to Parliament the rationale to enact more oppressive legislation against the American colonies.

"I hope a day may soon be appointed to consider the state of the nation with respect to America. I hope gentlemen will come to this debate with all the temper and impartiality that His Majesty recommends and the importance of the subject requires; a subject of greater importance than ever engaged the attention of this House, that subject only excepted when, near a century ago, it was the question whether you yourselves were to be bond or free. In the meantime, as I cannot depend upon my health for any future day—such is the nature of my infirmities—I will beg to say a few words at present, leaving the justice, the equity, the policy, the expediency of the act to another time.

"I will only speak to one point—a point which seems not to

have been generally understood. I mean to the *right*. Some gentlemen seem to have considered it as a point of honor. If gentlemen consider it in this light, they leave all measures of right and wrong, to follow a delusion that may lead to destruction. It is my opinion that this kingdom has no right to lay a tax upon the colonies. At the same time, I assert the authority of this kingdom over the colonies to be sovereign and supreme, in every circumstance of government and legislation whatsoever. They are the subjects of this kingdom, equally entitled with yourselves to all the natural rights of mankind and the peculiar privileges of Englishmen; equally bound by its laws and equally participating in the Constitution of this free country.

"The Americans are the sons, not the bastards, of England! Taxation is no part of the governing or legislative power!

"The taxes are a voluntary *gift* and *grant* of the Commons alone. In legislation the three estates of the realm are alike concerned; but the concurrence of the peers and the Crown to a tax is only necessary to clothe it with the form of a law. The gift and grant is of the Commons alone.

"In ancient days, the Crown, the barons, and the clergy possessed the lands. In those days, the barons and the clergy gave and granted to the Crown. They gave and granted what was *their own*! At present, since the discovery of America, and other circumstances permitting, the Commons are become the proprietors of the land. The Church—God bless it!—has but a pittance. The property of the Lords, compared with that of the Commons, is as a drop of water in the ocean; and this House represents those Commons, the proprietors of the lands; and those proprietors virtually represent the rest of the inhabitants. When, therefore, in this House we give and grant, we give and grant what is our own. But in an American tax, what do we do? 'We, your Majesty's commons for Great Britain, give and grant to Your Majesty'—what? Our *own* property? No! 'We give and grant to Your Majesty the property of your Majesty's Commons of America!' It is an absurdity in terms!

"The distinction between legislation and taxation is essentially necessary to liberty. The Crown and the peers are equally legislative powers with the Commons. If taxation be a part of simple *legislation*, then the Crown and the peers have rights in taxation as well as yourselves; rights which they *will* claim, which they *will* exercise, whenever the principle can be supported by power.

"There is an idea in some that the colonies are *virtually* represented in the House," said Pitt with a wryness that almost produced a grin on his face. "I would fain know *by whom* an American is represented here.

"Is he represented by any knight of the shire, in any county in this kingdom?" asked Pitt. "Would to God that respectable representation was augmented to a greater number! Or will you tell him that he is represented by any representative of a borough?—a borough which, perhaps, its own representatives never saw!" Pitt laughed once in dismissal of the idea. "*This* is what is called the rotten part of the Constitution! It cannot continue a century! If it does not drop, it must be amputated. The idea of a *virtual* representation of America in this House is the most contemptible idea that ever entered into the head of a man. It does not deserve a *serious* refutation.

"The Commons of America, represented in their several assemblies, have ever been in possession of the exercise of this their constitutional right of giving and granting their own money. They would have been slaves if they had not enjoyed it! At the same time, this kingdom, as the supreme governing and legislative power, has always bound the colonies by her laws, by her regulations, and restrictions in trade, in navigation, in manufactures, in everything, except that of taking their money out of their pockets without their consent.

"Gentlemen, sir, have been charged with giving birth to *sedition* in America. They have spoken their sentiments with freedom against this unhappy act, and that freedom has become their crime. Sorry I am to hear the liberty of speech in this

House imputed as a crime. But the imputation shall not discourage me. It is a liberty I mean to exercise. No gentleman ought to be afraid to exercise it. It is a liberty by which the gentleman who calumniates it might have profited. He ought to have desisted from his project. The gentleman tells us America is obstinate; America is almost in open rebellion. Well, I rejoice that America has resisted! Three millions of people, so dead to all the feelings of liberty as voluntarily to submit to be slaves, would have been fit instruments to makes slaves of the rest!

"Since the accession of King William, many ministers, some of great, others of more moderate abilities, have taken the lead of government. None of these thought, or even dreamed, of robbing the colonies of their constitutional rights. That was reserved to mark the era of the *late* administration. Not that there were wanting some, when I had the honor to serve His Majesty, to propose to me to burn my fingers with an American stamp act. With the enemy at their back, with our bayonets at their breasts, in the day of their distress, perhaps the Americans would have submitted to the imposition; but it would have been taking an ungenerous, an unjust advantage.

"The gentleman boasts of these bounties to America! Are not these bounties intended finally for the benefit of this kingdom? If not, he has misapplied the national treasures!

"I am no courtier of America, I stand up for this kingdom. I maintain that the Parliament has a right to bind, to restrain America! Our legislative power over the colonies is sovereign and supreme. When it ceases to be sovereign and supreme, I would advise every gentleman here to sell his lands, if he can, and embark for that country. When two countries are connected together like England and her colonies, without being incorporated, the one must necessarily govern. The greater must rule the less. But she must so rule as not to contradict the fundamental principles that are common to both.

"If the gentleman does not understand the difference between external and internal taxes, I cannot help it. There is a plain distinction between taxes levied for the purposes of raising a revenue and duties imposed for the regulation of trade, for the accommodation of the subject; although, in the consequences, some revenue may incidentally arise from the latter. The gentleman asks, when were the colonies *emancipated*? I desire to know, when were they made *slaves*?

"A great deal has been said without doors of the power, of the strength of America. It is a topic that ought to be cautiously meddled with. In a good cause, on a sound bottom, the force of this country can crush America to atoms. I know the valor of your troops, I know the skill of your officers. There is not a company of foot that has served in America out of which you may not pick a man of sufficient knowledge and experience to make a governor of a colony there. But on this ground, on the Stamp Act, which so many here will think a crying injustice, I am one who will lift up my hands against it! In such a cause, your success would be hazardous. America, if she fell, would fall like the strong man; she would embrace the pillars of the state, and pull down the Constitution along with her.

"Is this your boasted peace—not to sheathe the sword in its scabbard, but to sheathe it in the bowels of your countrymen? Will you quarrel with yourselves, now the whole house of Bourbon is united against you; while France disturbs your fisheries in Newfoundland, embarrasses your slave trade to Africa, and withholds from your subjects in Canada their property stipulated by treaty; while the ransom for the Manilas is denied by Spain, and its gallant conqueror basely traduced into a mean plunderer—a gentleman whose noble and generous spirit would do honor to the proudest grandee of that country?

"The Americans have not acted in all things with prudence and temper; they have been wronged; they have been driven to madness by injustice. Will you punish them for the madness you have occasioned? Rather let prudence and temper come first from *this* side. I will undertake for America that she will follow the example. There are two lines in a ballad of Prior's, of a man's behavior to his wife, so applicable to you and your colonies, that I cannot help repeating them:

> *'Be to her virtues very kind.*
> *Be to her faults a little blind'*

"Upon the whole, I will beg leave to tell the House what is my opinion. It is that the Stamp Act be repealed *absolutely, totally, and immediately!* And that the reason for the repeal be assigned—because it was founded on an erroneous principle. At the same time, let the sovereign authority of this country over the colonies be asserted in as strong terms as can be devised, and be made to extend to every point of legislation whatsoever; that we may bind their trade, confine their manufactures, and exercise every power whatsoever, except that of taking money from their pockets without consent."

Dogmael Jones's speech in Parliament for repeal of the Stamp Act answers objections to repeal and particularly William Pitt's pragmatic speech for repeal and tolerance.

"It is the anxious concurrence among the advocates of repeal and the defenders of the colonies here that some form of declaration of supremacy must accompany any act of repeal, for otherwise it is imagined, and not entirely without truth in the notion, that it would appear that the Crown, in such an act, would implicitly grant the colonies a unique state of political and economic independence not enjoyed by other Crown dominions.

"I join in that concurrence. For if the colonies are exempted from 'internal' legislative authority by Parliament, in little time it is supposed, also not entirely without justification, that they would begin to chafe under the proscriptions of the navigation laws and other constraints, and subsequently question that authority as well, and press for the immediate removal of those fetters.

"This is a true fear which I have often heard spoken in hushed words or delicate insinuations amongst both friends and foes of the colonies in this chamber. This fear may be credited, I am sorry to say, not to honest foresight, but to the natural apprehensions of frustrated and foiled political ambition and avarice.

"But, what have these gentlemen and lords to fear? I do not believe that the consequences of repeal by itself have occurred yet even to the most eloquent colonials, for, if the reports and testimony in this chamber are any guide, the most vocal and robust opposers of the Sugar and Stamp Acts there do not have political independence in mind so much as a fair and just regard by the Crown for their rights under our excellent constitution. An accompanying declaration of Parliamentary authority, if it comes to pass, will not much be noted by our fellow Britons over there. Only a few of them, and fewer of us, will see in such a sibling act the foundation of a more ruinous and angry contention than they believe the Crown is capable of handling, except in the manner of Turks.

"So, rather than seek to defend the temple of liberty, as many here purport to do, we will instead decide to prop up a moldy, half-collapsed, vine-smothered gazebo, which is infested with vermin and home to numerous rude and spiteful insects.

"Bind and confine the colonials? Should we not be honest about what this House intends to do? It is to bind and confine the colonials as captive felons, but take niggling, fussy care not to invade their pockets and appropriate what pittance is left to them after we have charged them the costs of their binding and confinement! What generosity! What kindness! What fairness! We propose to grant them the sanctity and liberty of their pockets, but not of their lives! But, should anyone in this House ever call this mode of supremacy *tyranny*, would he then be accused of treason?

"I wish to dwell for a moment on the unacknowledged, unspoken but common premise among all the speakers here, pro-repeal and anti-repeal alike, past and present, that the colonies are already 'another kingdom,' and that the alternatives open to them are mutually grim. Be warned: When that realization has occurred to our colonial brethren, the logic of their binding and confining circumstance must lead them inexorably to a choice, which is to decide whether to fight for their liberties as Englishmen, or as Americans for an independence that will better secure them those liberties, and not leave them to the invidious mercies of legislators across an ocean, as we propose to do here.

"I say again: For the Americans, the alternatives to repeal of the navigation laws, as well, beginning with repeal of the Stamp Act, ultimately will be war and independence, or war and conquest. Then the Americans must decide to fight, or to submit. If to fight, and possibly to win, this nation should feel no shame in having lost, for it will be credited with having birthed a giant. If to fight and be conquered by us, then they will simply rise up in another decade. And if to submit, then they will do so ignobly, bitterly, and shamefully, after all the stirring, memorable, and defiant words they had spoken. Then we will have won by default, we will have the colonies in thrall, and we will have a dubious revenue from them, but we should feel no pride *whatsoever* in that triumph.

"Fiat lux."

CHRONOLOGY OF ACTS OF PARLIAMENT
AND ROYAL DECREES CONCERNING
THE AMERICAN COLONIES, 1650-1775

Compiled by Edward Cline

1. Navigation Acts, October 1650, October 1651
    Forbade foreign ships from trading directly with English colonies, and required all ships to be English and crewed largely by English or American colonials.

2. Navigation Act, 1 October 1660 (confirmed in July 1661 on Restoration of Stuarts)
    Required all trade between Britain and colonies be conducted on English-built ships, with largely English crew.

3. Act of Frauds, 1662
    Only English-built ships could enjoy colonial trade.

4. Navigation Act, 1663
    Most European goods and commodities to be transshipped from England on English-built ships. Navy given responsibility for enforcing the Act.

5. Navigation Act, 1673
    Imposed tax or duty on colonial ships sailing between colonial

ports, and established customs commissioners to collect the duties.

6. Navigation Act, 1696
    Confined all colonial trade to English-built ships, gave colonial cus-
    toms officers same powers as English customs officers, required
    bonds on enumerated (regulated but not taxed) goods, expanded
    enforcement power of Navy, and voided all colonial laws contrary
    to all Navigation Acts.

7. Wool Act, 1699
    Restricted Irish woolen manufactures, and forbade export of
    American woolen products to England and between colonies.

8. Various Enumerated and Naval Stores Acts, 1705-1709
    Broadened number of enumerated commodities, and paid bounties
    (or "bonuses") on various products used in shipbuilding, espe-
    cially for Navy ships.

9. Beaver Skins, Furs, and Copper Ore, 1721
    Lowered duty on beaver skins, enumerated also furs and copper
    ore destined for Europe.

10. Hat Act, 1732
    Prohibited the export of colonial-made hats between colonies,
    regulated apprenticeships in hat-making, barred Negroes from
    apprenticeships.

11. Molasses Act, 1733
    Imposed prohibitive duties on rum, spirits, and molasses of foreign
    origin, except on British West Indies-produced molasses, rum, and
    spirits.

12. Iron Acts, 1750, 1757
    Forbade development of iron and steel industries in colonies, but
    (in 1757) allowed pig and iron bar imports to England duty-free.

13. Order in Council, 4 October 1763
    To combat colonial smuggling, to reform and strengthen the
    customs service in the colonies. Required Crown executives and
    officers to more aggressively enforce trade laws and customs
    regulations.

14. Proclamation, 7 October 1763
    Prohibited colonial settlement west of the Appalachians (or "trans-
    montane"), to regulate Indian trade, and to encircle the colonies to
    better regulate and tax them.

15. Revenue Act (or the Sugar Act, American Duties Act, or Duties
    Act), 5 April 1764
    To raise money to support the British army in the colonies.
    Reduced import tax on rum, molasses, and sugar from 6d to 3d per
    gallon. As an extention of the Molasses Act of 1733, intended to
    discourage smuggling of West Indies and Continental products.
    Established vice-admiralty court in Halifax to try offenders,
    indemnified customs officers from civil lawsuits in case of Crown
    loss of case. Created elaborate system of cockets, bonds, and per-
    mits to account for every item of merchandise on inland water
    transport and seaworthy vessels.

16. Currency Act, 19 April 1764
    Abolished and prohibited payment in colonial paper of debts to
    British creditors and merchants. Aimed at southern colonies, espe-
    cially Virginia, the largest debtor. This act only served to increase
    the indebtedness of the colonials, for most "specie" or hard money
    (coin) remained in Britain in consequence of the Navigation Act
    and other Crown mercantilist regulations.

17. Stamp Act, 22 March 1765
    Placed a stamp tax on virtually all legal and trade instruments at
    varying rates, payable in British specie only; added admiralty
    courts to enforce the Act in Philadelphia, Boston, and Charleston;

and abolished the Halifax court. Stamps also to be carried on pamphlets, newspapers, dice, and playing cards.

18. Quartering Act (or American Mutiny Act), 15 May 1765
Required colonial legislatures to victual and supply necessities to British troops housed in colonial barracks.

19. American Trade Act, 25 May 1765
Strengthened Revenue Act of 1764.

20. *Repeal of Stamp Act*, 18 March 1766
As a result of colonial protests, and consequent unenforceability of stamp tax collection. Georgia only colony to collect stamp tax.

21. Declaratory Act, 18 March 1766
Reaffirmed Parliamentary legislative authority over colonies "in all cases whatsoever."

22. Revenue Act, 6 June 1766
Created free ports in Jamaica and Dominica, reduced molasses duty to discourage smuggling, required bonds on all non-enumerated (or taxed) goods to the colonies or between colonies, and was intended to replace revenue lost by repeal of Stamp Act.

23. Revenue Act (or the Townshend Duties), 26 June 1767
Imposed tax on British-made paint, lead, paper, tea, and other items imported to colonies; legalized writs of assistance for customs searches; indemnified customs officers from lawsuits. Intended to subsidize colonial governments and British army.

24. Act for Creating American Board of Customs Commissioners, 29 June 1767
Intended to streamline customs administration and collection of various revenues.

25. Act for Suspending New York Assembly, 2 July 1767
    For the Assembly refusing to obey the Quartering Act of 1765.

26. Order in Council, 6 July 1768
    Reestablished Halifax admiralty court, and continuance of such
    courts in Boston, Philadelphia, and Charleston.

27. Parliamentary Resolves and address to king, 9 February 1769
    Reasserted right of Parliamentary authority over colonies; deemed
    resistance to said authority as treason, to be tried in England;
    deemed town meetings in Massachusetts as contrary to and apart
    from Crown authority.

28. *Repeal of Revenue or Townshend Act,* 12 April 1770
    Repealed all Townshend Act duties except the one on tea.

29. Act for Regulating India Tea, 27 April 1773
    Granted the British East India Company a monopoly on tea trade
    to the colonies.

30. Tea Act, 10 May 1773
    As sister act of the previous act, retained the duty on British East
    India Company tea shipped to the colonies. Intended to raise rev-
    enue and combat smuggling of Dutch tea.

31. Boston Port Act (the first "Intolerable" or "Coercive" Act),
    31 March 1774
    To punish Boston by closing its port until the £10,000 of tea
    destroyed during Boston Tea Party paid. Food and fuel exempted,
    and also military stores.

32. Massachusetts Government Act (an Intolerable Act), 20 May 1774
    Gave Crown-appointed governor broader powers of appointment
    over legislative approval; governor's council to be Crown-
    appointed, not elected; town meetings to have governor's prior

approval; and Crown to regulate juries.

33. Administration of Justice Ace (an Intolerable Act), 20 May 1774
    Permitted the removal of the trials of British officials charged with
    capital crimes to "friendlier" venues, i.e., outside of a colony's
    jurisdiction.

34. Quartering Act (an Intolerable Act), 2 June 1774
    British troops to be housed in vacant buildings if barracks not
    available.

35. Order in Council, October 1774
    Forbade arms imports to the colonies.

36. Quebec Act (an Intolerable Act), 22 June 1774
    Reaffirmed Crown authority over North America; redrew Quebec's
    boundaries, annexing all territory to Quebec province from St.
    Lawrence River to eastern banks of the Mississippi River to the
    Gulf of Mexico; and made Catholicism official religion of Quebec.

37. Order in Council, January 1775
    Empowered colonial governors to arbitrarily prorogue assemblies
    to prevent elections to Continental Congress.

38. Parliamentary Address to the king, 9 February 1775
    Claimed that a "state of war" existed between the Crown and the
    American colonies.

39. New England Restraining Act, 30 March 1775
    Stricter trade regulation enforcement of New England colonies,
    intended to harm trade.

40. Restraining Acts, 15 April 1775
    Stricter trade regulation enforcement of trade in Virginia, New
    Jersey, Maryland, Pennsylvania, and South Carolina.

41. Proclamation, 23 August 1775

    George III decreed a "state of rebellion and sedition" in the colonies, orders army to suppress rebellion and bring "traitors" to justice.

42. Proclamation, 26 October 1775

    George III conceded that American colonies are fighting for independence from the Crown, that a "state of war" exists, and charged peace commissioners to grant pardons and receive acknowledgment of Crown authority.

43. American Prohibitory Act, 22 December 1775

    Declared Americans "outlaws" and authorized seizure of American goods and ships. Pro-independence leaders in America and sympathetic members of Houses of Commons and Lords regard the Act as "independence by Act of Parliament." All American ports closed to British and foreign trade by 1 March 1776.

EIGHTEENTH–CENTURY BRITISH CURRENCY

by Edward Cline

In this period, all money, currency, or specie consisted of hard metal, in gold, silver, or copper denominations. Paper money, bank notes, or government-issued notes (from the Bank of England) were not much used because they were too easily susceptible to forgery and counterfeiting. The forerunner of today's paper money was a bill of exchange (q.v.) or a negotiable security, such as a console (a form of annuity), employed for convenience and efficiency of transaction and trade.

The American colonies were rarely granted the right to mint their own currency or specie; when they were, such colonial coin was not permitted to be used to pay debts to British creditors. As a consequence, to facilitate trade and to collect "internal" taxes within the colonies, colonial legislatures often resorted to issuing baseless paper money, which naturally depreciated over time and was subject to forgery and counterfeiting by colonial "false cambists."

Colonial trade with countries other than Britain brought in those countries' hard money, such as Spanish dollars and pistoles or German thalers, thus supplying a circulating medium of exchange within the colonies in lieu of scare British specie. It was the nature of the mercantilist system imposed on the colonies that British specie rarely came ashore in North America. Because the colonies were constantly in debt to the mother country, most "sterling" remained in the possession of British creditors and the taxing and regulatory authorities. Nevertheless, foreign money in the colonies had to be reckoned in terms of British specie.

* * *

GOLD COINS:	5-guinea; 2-guinea; guinea; and half guinea
SILVER COINS:	1 crown; half-crown; shilling; sixpence; 4-pence; 3-pence; 2-pence ("tuppence"); and the penny
COPPER COINS:	half-pence (also the "ha'penny"); the farthing

* * *

TABLE OF BRITISH SPECIE

4 Farthings = Penny or pence ("d")

$12d$ = Shilling ("s")

$2s, 6d$ = Half-crown

$5s$ = Crown

$20s$ = Pound ("£")

$13s, 4d$ = Mark

$21s$ = Guinea

A *SPARROWHAWK* GLOSSARY

Compiled by Edward Cline

Many fans of the *Sparrowhawk* series remark that while they enjoyed the story, they needed to keep a dictionary handy to find the meanings of many of the eighteenth–century terms encountered in the narrative and dialogue. With that "complaint" in mind, the *Companion* features a glossary of such terms. Most of the definitions below are the author's own, although some are taken from Samuel Johnson's 1755 *Dictionary*, while others are adapted from the *Oxford English Dictionary*. Other sources were *Haydn's Dictionary of Dates* (1881) and Richard Lederer Jr.'s *Colonial American English* (1985). The author kept employment of eighteenth–century terms to a minimum, but endeavored to balance their usage, especially in dialogue, with economy and clarity to evoke the period's spoken and written styles.

The glossary here is selective and does not claim to be exhaustive. In fact, a handful of terms, such as *embracery* and *barratry*, do not occur in the series at all. They are included because their meanings, bribery, and corruption respectively, are dramatized. Also, many classical Greek and Roman historical and mythological references that occur in the story have been omitted here, chiefly because I believe that sufficient contexts are established in the narrative and dialogue.

A

address In British politics, a document addressed to a monarch or legal body that supports or protests a specific government policy or instance of legislation. See MEMORIAL, PETITION, REMON-STRANCE.

advocate One who pleads for another, as in law; one who pleads for a cause or idea.

ague A fever marked by paroxysms of chills and sweating that recur at regular intervals; a fit of shivering.

Albion In the English version of the Greek legend, a son of Poseidon who taught men how to build ships; an ancient name for the British Isles.

arrack An alcoholic beverage made from coco sap or rice.

assize Periodical session of civil and criminal courts. See QUARTER SESSION.

attainder In eighteenth–century British law, the extinction of all civil and political rights after a sentence of treason, especially after a *bill of attainder*, which permitted the arrest and imprisonment of a person without the right of trial, was passed in legislation. The practice of attainders was much abused by political enemies, employed to neu-tralize or dispose of opponents. See GENERAL WARRANT, WRIT OF ASSISTANCE.

Attic salt Quickness and delicacy of wit; justness in taste; facility of conversation.

attorney One appointed or hired to act for another in business or legal matters; a qualified lawyer who represents clients in civil or crim-inal proceedings. See BAR, BARRISTER, SOLICITOR.

auto-da-fé Act of faith; the burning of a heretic, especially during the Inquisition.

B

bagnio 1. A public bath; 2. a brothel.

bailiff An officer of the court, under a sheriff, who executed writs and other legal documents; a warrant officer, pursuivant, or "catch-pole." See CATCHPOLE, CONSTABLE, SHERIFF.

bar The profession of barristers, the "bar" a railing that segregated a judge and presiding officers from the rest of a chamber or courtroom. See ATTORNEY, BARRISTER, SOLICITOR.

baron A member of the lowest order of nobility, in the eighteenth century nominally holding lands by leave or grant of the monarch. It was an alliance of barons that in 1215 forced King John of England to sign the Magna Carta. See DUKE, EARL, MARQUIS, VISCOUNT.

baronet A *petite* baron, below a baron and above a knight. See BARON, DUKE, EARL, MARQUIS, VISCOUNT.

barratry The trade in church or government appointments, or the selling of positions in the army, navy, and civil service. A regular source of political corruption in eighteenth–century England. See EMBRACERY.

barrister A lawyer called to the "bar" having the right to practice as an advocate in the superior courts. See ATTORNEY, BAR, SOLICITOR.

bashaw A "big" or important, powerful man (a corruption of the Hindu *pasha*).

battalion Two or more companies within an infantry regiment. See BRIGADE, COMPANY, REGIMENT.

beat to windward 1. To sail against the wind; 2. to oppose a trend, consensus or fashion. See also SOLDIER'S WIND.

bench A judge's seat, or the office of judge; a division of a higher court; collectively, judges and magistrates.

bencher A senior member of one of the Inns of Court who shared in management of an Inn. See INNS OF COURT.

benefit of clergy A condition of criminal sentencing, by which a defendant was granted a pardon if he could read, especially the Bible.

benefit of clergy, without A condition of criminal sentencing, regardless of a defendant's literacy.

big wig A gentleman, or member of the landed gentry. So called because of the more expensive perukes or wigs worn by this set.

bill 1. A quantity of printer's type, in various fonts, usually weighing 500 pounds; 2. a tabulation of charges for goods or services.

bill of exchange A commercial instrument, or a draft on a merchant's account, as good as currency, but based on credit; a written order to pay a sum to a drawer or to a named payee, usually dated.

bingo Brandy or other sweet alcohol.

blackleg A swindler.

blanc mange A dessert of opaque jelly of corn-flour and milk.

bottom 1. Courage; capacity to endure hardship; 2. that part of a vessel below its water line.

breakfast In the eighteenth century, a morning meal, taken about 8 o'clock. See DINNER, SUPPER.

brig A two-masted sailing ship, square-rigged on both masts, with two or more headsails and a quadrilateral gaff sail or spanker aft of the mizzenmast, and armed with ten to twelve guns. Brigs were often used as prisoner-of-war billets.

brigade An infantry unit usually consisting of three battalions. See BATTALION, COMPANY, REGIMENT.

brigantine A two-masted sailing ship, square-rigged on the foremast, having a for-and-aft mainsail with square main topsails.

bumbo A cheap drink of rum, sugar, and water. A variation was *bumpo*.

butt A barrel of beer or wine, equal to about two hogsheads. See HOGSHEAD, PUNCHEON.

C

caitiff A man of base, cowardly, or despicable character.

callidity Shrewdness.

cambist A dealer in bills of exchange, often forged or counterfeit.

canister An "encased" shot for close range artillery action. See CASE.

capon A domestic rooster, castrated and fattened for food.

carcass An incendiary shell fired by naval or land artillery containing embers designed to explode on an enemy vessel or position to start a fire. See SABOT.

case An artillery munition, consisting of bagged musket shot the size of marbles, designed to inflict maximum casualties. See CANISTER, GRAPE.

casuist 1. A theologian or ombudsman who resolves questions of duty, conscience, and related moral matters; 2. a sophist or quibbler.

catchpole A constable or bailiff, especially one who arrests for debt. See BAILIFF, CONSTABLE, SHERIFF, WATCHMAN.

chamade A military drum signal calling for a parley between opposing forces.

Chancery A court of equity in the civil court system. See INNS OF COURT.

chap In the seventeenth and eighteenth centuries, a term of mild contempt for a stranger or intruder.

chapbook A cheap, small book (usually 15-24 pages) that contained news, laws, and folk wisdom, which sold for a penny.

chapman An itinerant purveyor of miscellaneous wares, including chapbooks, in rural England. See HIGGLER.

chilblain(s) A malady marked by the itching or swelling of a hand or foot, caused by exposure to the cold and poor circulation.

chocolate pot A pot of either copper or salt-glazed stoneware for serving hot chocolate.

cockalorum 1. A self-important little man; 2. a children's game like leapfrog.

cocket A customs house certificate of specifically labeled and destined goods on board a merchant ship. See DOCKET, DUTY, MANIFEST.

cogger A flatterer, a wheedler. "To cog: to lie, to wheedle." (Samuel Johnson's *Dictionary*) A variation is *codger*.

Cogita mori "Think upon death." (Latin)

Common Pleas In eighteenth– and nineteenth–century Britain, a superior or supreme court whose venue was fixed in 1215 at Westminster Hall. Until then, like the King's Bench, it sat wherever the monarch happened to be. See KING'S BENCH.

company 1. A social term for a group of guests; 2. in the eighteenth-century British army, a unit consisting of one captain, two lieutenants, two sergeants, three corporals, one drummer, and thirty-eight privates, or a full company. See BATTALION, BRIGADE, REGIMENT.

coney A rabbit; fur from this animal ("coney wool").

constable An officer (municipal or parish) of a county, parish, or township appointed to act as conservator of the peace and to perform a number of public administrative duties. See BALIFF, CATCHPOLE,

SHERIFF.

copyhold The right to farm leased or rented land for one or more life-times within a family. The father was usually the *copyholder*. A copyhold was usually passed on to the eldest son. See ENTAIL, PRIMO-GENITURE.

cornet 1. The standard or colors of a troop of cavalry; 2. The fifth commissioned officer in a troop of cavalry, who carried the colors, corresponding to an ensign in the army. See ENSIGN.

count A foreign nobleman corresponding to the rank of earl. The French style is *comte*.

Country-dance From the French *contradance*. A popular group dance of several couples in Britain and the American colonies. The fore-runner of the American "square dance."

crack A prostitute. See FIRESHIP.

crack lay A burglary in which force is used to enter a house. See DUB LAY, RUM LAY.

cresset An iron basket fitted to a pole in which pitch pine was burned to serve as street lighting or a source of warmth.

crimp To trap or entrap into military service; a person who entraps or forces a man into naval or army service. Eighteenth–century recruiting sergeants and officers were paid a bonus for each man who enlisted in Britain's volunteer army. The navy, however, resorted to and relied upon impressment to fill its ranks. See IMPRESSMENT.

crimping house A house used by army recruiters to house recruits until they are sent to their regiments. See CRIMP.

crop note A receipt issued by colonial tobacco inspectors listing a planter's hogsheads by mark and number; the gross, net, and tare weights of the tobacco; and specifying whether it was sweetscented or Oronoco, stemmed or leaf. In the American colonies, a crop note could be used as currency to purchase goods or pay debts. See TARE, TRANSFER NOTE.

currency Coin or bank notes. See DOLLAR, GUINEA, HALF-JOE, POUND, SPECIE.

custom A duty or tax on foreign imported goods. Distinct from an excise tax. See EXCISE, TARIFF.

D

daggle To splash with water and mud, or to run through muddy water.

device The forerunner of a trademark, usually a combination of a planter's initials and a unique symbol that identified a planter's hogshead of tobacco. See also PLANTER.

disseise In law, to wrongfully deprive or dispose of property or life.

dinner In the eighteenth century, the main meal taken in midday, around 2 o'clock. See BREAKFAST, SUPPER.

dissolve In government, the act of an executive, such as a colonial governor or Britain's monarch, to end a legislative session. See PROROGUE.

docket A warrant from a customs house certifying that duties have been paid on imported goods. See COCKET, DUTY, MANIFEST.

dog-cart A two-wheeled cart with cross seats back-to-back (originally used to carry dogs).

dollar A Spanish milled silver coin, used in the colonies in lieu of scarce British hard currency, with a value of between two shillings sixpence and four and sixpence. The term first occurs in Shakespeare's *Macbeth*. (From the Dutch *daler*, or German *thaler*.) See PISTOLE, SPECIE.

Dover's powder An eighteenth–century patent medicine of opium and the ipecacuanha root, taken or administered for almost any pain.

dragoon A mounted infantryman.

drawback In the eighteenth–century mercantilist system, a duty paid on imported goods, remitted or returned as a rebate to an importer when the goods have been cleared for re-export. In the eighteenth–century, tobacco planters were required to send their tobacco to Britain on British vessels, and were taxed for the "import" to Britain. Most tobacco imports were sent on to the Continent. British agents who stored the tobacco for re-export credited the planters' accounts with the rebated duties.

Droit of Admiralty 1. The proceeds or booty from a captured enemy vessel; 2. colloquially, a wreck's cargo claimed or seized by civilians living on a coast.

drum A tea party, so called because the tea was served on a drum table.

dub lay A burglary in which keys are used to enter a house. See also CRACK LAY, RUM LAY.

Duck Lane An eighteenth–century London street noted for its book-sellers.

duffer An accomplice in tea smuggling, who sold untaxed tea to street hawkers or house to house.

duke The highest hereditary title of nobility; a sovereign prince who rules a duchy or small state; a royal prince. See BARON, BARONET, EARL, MARQUIS, VISCOUNT.

dulcify 1. To sweeten naturally acidic or bitter food; 2. to flatter.

dun To demand payment of a bill or debt; to take legal action against a debtor.

duty An impost or customs tax recoverable by law on goods imported, exported, or consumed. See CUSTOMS, EXCISE, TARIFF.

E

earl A nobleman ranking between a marquis (variation: *marquess*) and viscount. See BARON, BARONET, DUKE, MARQUIS, VISCOUNT.

embracery The crime of bribery. See BARRATRY.

encomium A formal essay marked by high-blown praise of, or glowing tribute to an author that introduced his book. It is now called a *preface* or *introduction*, and is more likely today to be more instructive, informative, and even objective.

English mobility The common people, or the mob. See MOB.

ensign In the eighteenth century, the lowest-ranking army officer (today a subaltern), corresponding to a CORNET in the cavalry, usually charged with minor command duties and with carrying a regiment's colors; the regimental colors.

entail The custom or legally mandated practice of preserving a land estate so that it may pass on to a father's first-born or eldest son. See COPYHOLD, PRIMOGENITURE.

epergne A serving platter of several levels or tiers for holding desserts, fruits, and sweetmeats.

esquire The title of gentry, immediately below a BARON or knight. In medieval times, a *squire* was a knight's valet.

excise A duty or tax levied on goods or commodities produced or sold within a country, and also on various licenses. See CUSTOM, TARIFF.

F

fair-trader A "legitimate" merchant who paid all customs and excise taxes. See FREE-TRADER.

false cambist A counterfeiter or forger of paper currency and bills of exchange. See CAMBIST, CURRENCY, SPECIE.

faro A "banking" game in which players bet on cards drawn from a dealing box.

fathom A nautical term for a depth of six feet.

fatwit A dull, stupid person, made more so by strong drink.

firelock A smooth-bore, muzzle-loading musket. See WALLGUN.

fireship 1. A damaged naval vessel set afire and sent in the direction of enemy ships or so placed to deter pursuit or further engagement; 2. a prostitute with venereal disease. See CRACK.

flapper A stranger who seems familiar to one.

flagitious Deeply criminal, or utterly villainous.

flimflam An idle, usually untrue story.

flip Strong beer sweetened with molasses and dried pumpkin; also a measure of rum.

flummery Confusing nonsense.

fly Sharp-witted.

footman A liveried servant who rode on the rear of a coach or carriage.

footpad A stealthy robber who worked on foot.

fopdoodle A fool. "An insignificant wretch." (Samuel Johnson's *Dictionary*)

fowling piece A gaming flintlock musket that fired buckshot, a precursor of the shotgun.

free-trader The self-styled name of British smugglers of untaxed goods, especially in the south counties. See FAIR-TRADER.

frigate A three-masted naval vessel, smaller than a ship of the line, but as large or larger than a merchantman, having only one gun deck, or between 20 and 36 guns. The *Sparrowhawk* is a fifth-rate frigate, converted to a merchantman, whose guns were placed "on deck" to make room for cargo below decks.

fuddle To intoxicate, stupefy, or confuse a person with drink or sophistry; a spell of drinking.

funky Ill-smelling.

fusil 1. A "light" musket, carried by officers; 2. a grenadier's grenade fuse or match.

fusilier Originally, a grenadier who accompanied artillery trains, but by the mid-eighteenth century a grenadier who carried a fusil. See GRENADIER.

fustian 1. A bombastic, florid type of prose, consisting of "words and ideas ill-associated" (Samuel Johnson's *Dictionary*); 2. a strong cotton and linen fabric.

G

galley A ship's boat, propelled by oarsmen, large enough to carry several men. See GIG, JOLLY-BOAT.

gavotte A lively version of the minuet, often performed by two or more couples.

general warrant In the eighteenth century, a "discretionary" power of the British government, exercised by secretaries of state, to apprehend and arrest persons chiefly for seditious libel, but also for other "suspect" actions perceived as endangering the state or the sovereign. Much abused by political officials, especially as a device to impose censorship on writers and printers, the most famous victim of one was John Wilkes in 1763. Chief Justice Pratt of the Common Pleas declared general warrants unconstitutional in 1766, while Chief Justice Mansfield of the King's Bench upheld them. See ATTAINDER, WRIT OF ASSISTANCE.

gibbet A cage-like iron box, supported by a pole, erected near a public way or the scene of a crime, in which a hanged or executed criminal was displayed.

gig 1. A light, two-wheeled, one-horse carriage; 2. a ship's boat, propelled by oarsmen, used for communicating between vessels at sea or between ship and port, but usually employed to convey a ship's captain or naval commander. See GALLEY, JOLLY-BOAT.

gillie A man or boy attending a Scottish sportsman or chief; a shotgun bearer.

gin A corruption of "Geneva" from Holland, distilled from grain or malt, flavored with juniper. Gin was the most affordable alcohol to the lower classes, even when taxed.

gorget In medieval times, a piece of armor that protected a knight's throat; in the eighteenth century, an ornamental, embossed, roughly crescent-shaped plate of brass or coated tin, secured by a chain or cord, signifying officer status and "knighthood."

grape An artillery munition, consisting of clusters of iron balls roughly the size of golf balls, intended to inflict maximum casualties. See CANISTER, CASE.

grasshopper A British three-pound gun often attached to a regiment. See GUN.

grenadier A soldier who threw hand grenades, lit by his fusil. British, French, and Prussian grenadiers were also chosen for their extraordinary height (usually six feet). See FUSILIER.

grocer A wholesaler of foodstuffs (from *gross*).

gudgeon A dupe or a fool.

guinea An English gold coin of 21 shillings, which circulated between 1663 and 1817. It was replaced with the pound. A pound weighed twenty shillings. See POUND, SHILLING.

gun Any army or naval artillery piece, distinguished from small arms such as pistols, firelocks (*muskets*), and, later, rifles, all of the later often referred to as *side-arms*.

H

H.M.S. His or Her Majesty's ship, the prefix for Royal Navy vessel names, not adopted, however, until 1789, at the outset of Britain's conflict with France. The prefix was adopted probably as a reaction to the French Revolution, to stress that England was a monarchy.

halberd A spear-like staff, largely ceremonial, topped with an elaborately forged ax instead of a spear tip, carried by sergeants in eighteenth–century armies.

Half-Joe A Portuguese gold coin (a Johannes) worth 36 shillings.

Halifax gibbet A device for beheading, the forerunner of the French guillotine.

hand A bundle of tobacco leaves, packed together with other hands in the packing or "prizing" of a hogshead. See HOGSHEAD.

Harry 1. A country man, or a rustic; 2. to harass, pursue, or investigate.

hazard A game of chance, similar to craps, played with two dice.

hick A country man or rustic; an ignorant clown.

higgler A dealer in or carrier of sundry dry goods. See CHAPMAN.

hogshead A cask or barrel constructed to hold between 700 and 1,400 pounds of tobacco, and also used to transport grain. See BUTT, HAND, PUNCHEON.

Holland See GIN.

House of Commons The lower governing and legislative body of the British Parliament. In the eighteenth century, its elective members often numbered over 600. Many blocs of seats were controlled by members of the House of Lords, as well as by the sovereign, as a check on the "democratic" tendencies of the Commons, or to introduce or ensure passage of certain bills. Army and Navy officers, as well as civilians, also held seats in the Commons. The Commons reserved the power to originate money or finance bills, and also tax legislation.

House of Lords The upper governing and legislative body of the British Parliament. In the eighteenth century, its membership numbered about 240, including many bishops. Only peers, either hereditary or elevated by the sovereign, could sit in Lords. Lords also acted as the "supreme court" of Britain, when a peer was charged with a capital crime (treason or murder). In practice, Lords functioned as a modern "senate." It could reject or pass by vote any money or finance bill sent up from the Commons, and also tax legislation.

howitzer An artillery gun used to throw balls over an enemy's fortifications.

hundred A subdivision of some English shires and colonial American counties. See WAPENTAKE.

hurdy-gurdy A mechanical, violin-like musical instrument that could play melodies set by devices in the neck.

I

impressment The practice of the British navy in the eighteenth and early ninteenth centuries of raiding chiefly port towns to kidnap men to serve in involuntary servitude on warships. The raiding parties were called *press gangs* or *pressmen*. See CRIMP.

in case A colonial planter's term for a tobacco leaf's time for handling, the leaf being neither dry enough to crumble nor damp enough to begin rotting, and ready for packing or prizing into a hogshead. See HAND, HOGSHEAD.

in fee A baron's proprietaryship of a king's land in exchange for an oath of loyalty and obedience, together with the obligation to provide the king with a fixed number of knights and common soldiers for military service. This legal device was linked closely to the notion of "quit-rents," in which a landowner paid the monarch a "rent" in exchange for an exemption from all other royal obligations. See QUIT-RENT, SOCCAGE.

indenture A state of contractual or criminal servitude, in which one's labor is committed or leased for a specified period of time, in the eighteenth century, usually seven years, under penalty of criminal infraction. See REDEMPTIONER.

indigo A plant cultivated for blue dye.

Inns of Court The several legal societies or "colleges" having the exclusive right to teach law and admit persons to practice at the bar. See ATTORNEY, BAR, BARRISTER, BENCHER, CHANCERY.

interlude A dramatic or comedic stage production, technically not a play, and staged without the lord chamberlain's license. The Licensing Act of 1737 for decades gave Drury Lane and Covent Garden in London a near monopoly on full stage play productions. The Act was intended to forestall ridicule of unpopular public figures, such as prime minister Robert Walpole, and to preserve "public decency and morals."

ironmonger A dealer in ironware; a hardware merchant.

J

Jack Ketch A colloquialism for the hangman.

javelin men A body of men in a sheriff's retinue who carried spears or pikes, and escorted the judges at the assizes. They also escorted convicts to their execution or place of public punishment. See CONSTABLE, SHERIFF.

jolly-boat A ship's boat, propelled by oarsmen, smaller than a cutter. The origin of *jolly* is unknown. Possibly it is a slang corruption of the French *joie* for the delight or gladness felt by naval or civilian seamen when they were rowed ashore in it to spend leave in a port town. See GALLEY, GIG.

jointure An estate settled on a wife to be taken by her in lieu of a dowry; a settlement on the wife of a freehold estate for her lifetime.

Jonathan (Brother) A British nickname for America or an American.

jougs An iron neck ring or collar, with a joint or hinge in back to permit opening and closing, and loops in front for a padlock, worn by offenders in England and Scotland.

K

ketch A small vessel with one large mast, usually with a triangular sail.

kickshaw A fancy food dish, usually a "dainty" French concoction, elegant but insubstantial.

King's Bench In Britain, until 1875, a superior or supreme court that could hear major criminal and civil cases. (In Queen Victoria's time, it was the *Queen's Court*.) Its name is derived from the bench on which a monarch sat when a case required his attendance. The King's Bench could sit wherever a monarch happened to be, when necessary. Like the Court of the Common Pleas, it had its own chief justice. See COMMON PLEAS.

knacker 1. A shipbreaker, or one who takes apart or breaks up a vessel; 2. a buyer of dilapidated buildings for their usable materials;

3. to break up an unwieldy sentence.

knocking shop A brothel. "Knocking" was likely a euphemism for an expletive.

L

lamb's wool A drink consisting of hot ale mixed with the pulp of roasted apples, sugar, and spice.

larboard The "port" side of a vessel, on the left side looking forward. (*Port side* did not come into common usage until 1846).

larrikin A hoodlum or rowdy.

league Three English or nautical miles.

levee 1. A reception held by a person of distinction on rising from bed; 2. an afternoon assembly at which a sovereign, lord or his proxy received only men; 3. a reception held in honor of a particular person.

Lewis Or *Ludwig*, the family name of the Hanoverians, beginning with George the First.

livery 1. The distinctive attire of a servant; 2. a stable for horses, where they could be billeted or hired.

logodædaly Cleverness in wordplay.

loo A card game, a forerunner of bridge.

lord 1. Feudal superior; 2. a nobleman, peer of the realm entitled by courtesy to the title or address of "Lord." The Scottish style was *laird*.

lunge To exercise and train a horse in a wide circle with the aid of a long rope.

lurdane A lazy, stupid person.

lustre A chandelier of crystal and polished silver, whose reflecting properties aided in amplifying candlelight.

M

majesty The person of a sovereign, used in address to a king, queen, emperor, or empress; a royal bearing or aspect.

manifest A merchantman's cargo list of goods carried on the vessel. See COCKET, DOCKET, DUTY.

mar(ling) To mix clay and lime into arable soil in order to improve its fertility.

market town Since medieval times, a town legally permitted to hold an open-air market of producers and buyers.

marle A soft, soapy earth found from between 18 inches to several feet below ground surface.

marquis A noble rank between a duke and an earl (wife: *marchioness*). A variation is *marquess*. See BARON, BARONET, DUKE, EARL, VISCOUNT.

masquerade A social gathering of persons wearing masks or dominos and often fantastic costumes. Also called a *mask* or *masque*.

master 1. One having authority over another; 2. a youth or boy too young to be addressed "mister," "sir," or "lord"; 3. the eldest son of a Scottish viscount or baron.

memorial A statement of facts, addressed to a government (in Britain, to the House of Lords), often accompanied by a petition or remonstrance. See ADDRESS, PETITION, REMONSTRANCE.

Mendips A range of hills noted for limestone caves near the southwest coast of England.

mercer A dealer in small wares.

merchant An importer and exporter of goods in quantity.

merchantman A British commercial vessel, especially a seagoing one.

milord An Englishman of noble or genteel birth; the address of such a person, instead of "sir."

mob The fickle crowd, a contraction of *mobile vulgus* (Latin); a further pun on *English mobility* (q.v.), which was a humorous opposition to the "nobility" (*nob* or *nab*).

Mohock An aristocratic bully or hoodlum, thug, or tough, who wandered about London with a gang of his ilk to terrorize or torment at whim. Also called a *tumbler* or *sweater*.

moonraker An illusory thing or idea; a person who has illusory ideas or behaves oddly. Its origin was the practice of raking the reflection of the moon from a pool of water.

mortar A short, large-bore cannon for throwing shells (lit-fuse explosives) in high trajectories to fall on or behind enemy fortifications.

N

nab A satirical, deprecating address for *his worship, his lordship*, and so on. Its usual form was *his nabs* or *his nibs*. Possibly a corruption of the Hindu *nabob*.

nailery An ironworks.

nautical mile One minute of longitude, or 6,000 feet. See LEAGUE.

necessary An outdoor lavatory.

nice Minutely accurate; over-refined.

niffy-naffy A silly fellow; a trifler.

noddy A simpleton; foolish.

nonage The state of being under legal age; one's minority; immaturity.

nonce 1. For the time being; 2. a word coined for the occasion.

O

oat The primary grain of Scotland and northern England, used in the preparation of haggis, oatcake, porridge, and horse feed.

orangery Originally, in the Restoration era, a room that sheltered orange trees, but which later became a sun room and breakfast room.

ordinary 1. An unembellished inn for travelers, atop a tavern; 2. a diocesan officer appointed to give criminals their "neck-verses" (before hanging), and to prepare them for death; 3. the chaplain of a prison, whose duty it was to prepare condemned prisoners for death.

Oronoco A species of tobacco plant, the rival of sweetscented tobacco, with coarser leaves, and, when smoked, with a more pungent taste and odor. Introduced from the Oronoco River basin in South America.

orrery An apparatus showing the relative positions and motions of planets and their moons in the solar system, employing an integrated wheelworks that set the system in motion. After Charles Boyle, 4th Earl of Orrery (1676-1731).

overlooker On a plantation, a man who supervised overseers, sharing the duties of a steward. See OVERSEER, PLANTER, STEWARD.

overseer On a plantation, a man responsible for carrying out tasks, and managed slaves and servants.

own Acknowledge, admit, concede, or confess a thing.

oyer and terminer Sessions of court held by circuit judges for capital offenses. See ASSIZE, QUARTER SESSION.

P

parish lamp The most common form of street lighting in mid-eighteenth century London and other British cities, fueled with whale blubber, and the responsibility of parishes.

Parliament The supreme governing and legislative body of Britain, composed of the upper house (Lords) and the lower, elective house (the Commons). Its executive was the monarch, who could veto or endorse legislation passed by both houses. See HOUSE OF COMMONS, HOUSE OF LORDS.

parky A cold or chilly condition. Said also of weather or a person's character.

peer A member of one of the degrees of nobility. Possibly an Anglicism of the French *per* (connoting *father* or seniority). A peer was a *baron,* an *earl,* a *marquis,* a *viscount,* or a *duke.*

peruke A man's wig, made of human or horse hair.

petition In British politics, a document stating a grievance or grievances signed by a certain number of bona fide individuals, requesting redress, addressed to a sovereign or government body. In the eighteenth century, it was usually addressed to the Commons. See ADDRESS, MEMORIAL, REMONSTRANCE.

phaeton A light, four-wheeled, uncovered carriage, pulled by two horses. See POST-CHAISE.

phiz Slang for face. Probably a corruption of *visage.*

phiz-monger An artist who painted the faces of portraits, leaving assistants or apprentices to paint the bodies, clothes, backgrounds, and so on.

phlogiston Before the discovery of oxygen by Joseph Priestly, a substance thought to reside in all inflammable matter and released during combustion.

pillory A device for publicly punishing criminal offenders, consisting of a wooden frame with holes for the head and hands. An offender stood on a pillory. See STOCKS.

pipe 1. A device for smoking tobacco, in the eighteenth century, usually made of clay; 2. a 100-gallon cask of spirits.

pippin 1. Any of a variety of apples valued for their dessert quality; 2. a highly esteemed or very admirable person or thing.

pistole A Spanish gold coin, worth sixteen shillings and nine pence, which circulated in the colonies in lieu of scarce British specie or money. See DOLLAR, SPECIE.

planter A tobacco plantation owner (from the practice of replanting tobacco seedlings from seedbeds to separate mounds).

Pleiad A group of seven illustrious or brilliant persons or things, in reference to a cluster of stars in the constellation Taurus.

plumb A slang expression to describe a person worth at least £100,000 sterling.

point In grammar and composition, to punctuate.

pony The sum of fifty guineas (£52.5).

porter A dark, heavy beer. Also called *stout*.

posset A drink of hot milk, curdled with ale or wine, flavored with spices, used as a remedy for colds or minor ailments.

post-chaise A two-wheeled, horse-drawn conveyance with a hood, for two persons. See PHAETON.

postilion A liveried servant who rode on the lead horse of a team-drawn coach, in place of a coachman or driver.

pound A gold coin of twenty shillings, adopted in 1813 to replace the guinea. Symbol: £. The pound later became the *sovereign*. See DOLLAR, GUINEA, SPECIE, STERLING.

powder monkey In all eighteenth–century navies, a boy who brought up charges from the magazine for naval guns.

prat The buttocks, slang since the seventeenth century for a fool.

priming 1. The removal from tobacco plants of undesirable leaves that allegedly deprived desired leaves of nutrition and water; 2. to load a musket or firelock by assembling the bullet.

primogeniture The custom or legally mandated practice of passing land ownership from father to the first-born or eldest son. See COPY-HOLD, ENTAIL.

prize To pack harvested tobacco into a hogshead. Possibly a corruption of *press*.

prorogue The power of an executive, such as a colonial governor, to delay or postpone a legislative session. See DISSOLVE.

puncheon A large cask or barrel for liquids, especially for alcohol, of between seventy-two and 120 gallons. See BUTT, HOGSHEAD.

Q

quahog An edible round clam found on the Atlantic coast, the shells of which were often used as gravel on colonial streets. Ground up, it was also used as fertilizer.

Quaker After the pacifist religious sect, a log fashioned and painted to pass for a naval gun, in order to deceive an enemy about a vessel's fire power.

quarter session A court of limited criminal and civil jurisdiction, and of appeal, held quarterly. The British terms or sessions were Michaelmas, Hilary, Easter, and Trinity. See ASSIZE.

Queer Street The state of bankruptcy.

queue A "pigtail" attached to a man's wig or hair, bound by a ribbon over the back of his neck.

quillet A verbal nicety or subtle distinction. Probably from *quillet*, a small, narrow strip of land.

quit-rent A fee or "rent" paid to a lord or sovereign by a freeholder or copyholder in lieu of military or other service. See IN FEE, SOCCAGE.

R

redemptioner An immigrant whose passage to America was paid for by a merchant, and who indentured his labor until the cost of the passage was redeemed by either the merchant or his employer.

regiment In the British army, a unit of about 475 men, organized into ten companies. See BATTALION, BRIGADE, COMPANY.

remembrancer One of several English officials originally appointed to remind a sovereign or government official of a duty, or to collect debts owed the sovereign.

remonstrance In British politics, a document addressed to the Commons formally stating pointed opposition or a grievance. See ADDRESS, MEMORIAL, PETITION.

Rex Anglias English king (Latin), meaning an English sovereign.

Rex Anglorum King of the English (Latin), meaning a non-English sovereign.

rhino Cash, specie, currency.

ridge A guinea. See POUND, STERLING.

riding chair In colonial America, a conveyance similar to a sulky. See SULKY.

riditto A masquerade. See MASQUERADE.

right To be compliant, willing.

royal foot scamp A footpad or robber who robbed with civil manners. See SCAMP.

royal scamp A mounted "gentleman" highwayman, who robbed with manners. See SCAMP.

ruelle A reception held in the bedchamber of a fashionable lady.

rum lay The art of burglary of private residences. See CRACK LAY, DUB LAY.

rummage 1. To make either a thorough or haphazard search, especially by customsmen of a merchantman to find untaxed, smuggled rum, and later for any contraband or untaxed or illegal goods; 2. to examine minutely and completely.

runagate A vagabond. Probably a corruption of *renegade* (one who runs or flees).

S

sabot In naval munitions, a wooden or metal device that contained incendiary materials fired at an enemy vessel (from the French for *shoe*). See CARCASS.

scamp A highwayman, or armed robber, mounted or on foot. See TOBY.

scope An aim or purpose.

seegar A roll of tobacco leaf, smoked in lieu of a pipe. Now a *cigar*.

sheriff An officer of a county charged with judicial duties such as executing processes and orders of courts and judges. (From OE *shire reeve*.) See BAILIFF, CONSTABLE.

ship's husband A joint-stock owner of a merchantman chosen by other stockholders to supervise the building, fitting, and sailing of a ship, and also to keep accounts.

ship of the line A warship of two or three gun decks, of between sixty and 120 guns.

Simurg In Persian mythology, a monstrous bird having the powers of reasoning and speech. See WYVERN.

slip slop "Bad liquor." (Samuel Johnson's *Dictionary*)

sloop A small, one-masted fore-and-aft rigged vessel with a mainsail and jib; a sloop-of-war with ten guns on the upper deck.

slops A sailor's loose, knee-length knickerbockers. A forerunner of *pantaloons*, or *pants*.

slubberdegullion "A paltry, dirty, sorry wretch." (Samuel Johnson's *Dictionary*)

smack A single-masted sailing boat for coasting or fishing.

small beer A trivial matter or concern.

smallclothes A man's close-fitting, knee-length breeches.

snollygoster A shrewd, unscrupulous person.

soccage A feudal tenure of land requiring payment of rent or other non-military service to a lord or sovereign. See COPYHOLD, IN FEE, QUIT-RENT.

soldier's wind A wind "on the beam"; to sail with the wind. See BEAT TO WINDWARD.

solicitor 1. A member of the legal profession qualified to advise clients and instruct barristers, but barred from appearing as an advocate in court except in certain lower courts; 2. a law officer below an attorney-general. See ATTORNEY, BARRISTER.

soul driver A colonial middleman who purchased transported felons and redemptioners and drove them to market in the Tidewater and Piedmont of Virginia.

sparrowhawk Any of various small hawks or falcons in Europe and North America.

specie Coined money. See DOLLAR, POUND, STERLING.

sponge To defraud or cheat.

sponger A prison for debtors. Also a *sponging house*.

spontoon A spear-like staff, largely ceremonial, carried by officers in eighteenth–century armies.

spouting club A London club for those interested in public address, usually meeting in a tavern or public house.

starboard The right side of a vessel, looking forward. See LAR-BOARD.

sterling 1. British silver money, of 92.5 percent purity; 2. of solid, impeccable worth.

steward On a plantation, the man who oversaw agricultural tasks, supervising overseers, and was responsible for provisioning the master's or owner's house with food and other necessities.

stocks A wooden frame with holes for a prisoner's legs and/or hands, into which the prisoner would be locked for public punishment. See PILLORY.

stone For centuries, the official British unit of weight, equal to four-teen pounds.

subaltern The military rank of an officer below that of captain. See ENSIGN.

sucker To remove new shoots from a tobacco stalk.

sulky A two-wheeled, one-horse carriage for one person, canopy optional. See RIDING CHAIR.

supper In the eighteenth century, a main meal taken in the evening, about 8 o'clock. See BREAKFAST, DINNER.

sweating The humidification of cured tobacco leaves to attain plia-bility.

sweetscented A species of tobacco with fine leaves and a mild taste. See ORONOCO.

syllabub A dessert made of cream or milk, curdled with wine and sometimes with whipped or solidified gelatin.

T

tardle An entanglement, or complicated situation.

tare An allowance made for the weight of a hogshead (or other con-tainer) in which tobacco was prized or packed, e.g., 1097 pounds gross minus 979 pounds net equals 118 pounds tare. See CROP NOTE, TRANSFER NOTE.

tariff A tax levied on goods or commodities imported into a country for final sale, used as a revenue-raising device or as a political policy to either protect a country's industry or as a penalty to discourage consumption of a commodity. See CUSTOM, EXCISE.

tatler A clock or watch.

tilbury Sixpence. Formerly the fare for crossing by boat on the Thames River between Gravesend and Tilbury Fort.

tipstaff A sheriff's officer, bailiff, or constable; an officer who waited on a court. So called because of the iron-tipped staff he carried.

tobo Shorthand for tobacco, an abbreviation used in account book entries.

toby A colloquial term for a highway or road as a regular venue of robbery. *High* toby was robbery committed by a mounted robber; *low* toby was committed by footpads. See SCAMP.

ton A prevailing fashion or vogue. From the French *tone*.

top sail To abandon one's debts by going to sea.

topping The pruning of undressed, unwanted tobacco leaves from a stalk.

Tory A member of a British political group that originally supported the Stuarts, and later royal authority and the established (state) church, and that opposed all Parliamentary reforms. From the Irish-Gaelic term *toraidhe*, a pursued man, robber or outlaw. See WHIG.

toy An amusing or diverting thing.

toy shop A shop in which baubles and trifles were sold.

transfer note A receipt from a colonial tobacco inspector for a certain number of pounds of loose, un-prized tobacco, and which, like the crop note, could be used as currency to purchase goods, but not for payment of debts outside of the colonies. See CROP NOTE, TARE.

turn off To hang or execute a criminal.

U

union A group of English country parishes consolidated for the administration of the poor laws.

uphills Loaded dice, or dice that were weighted to turn up high numbers.

V

vail A gratuity or tip.

vestry In the Anglican Church, a committee of members of a parish that administered parish affairs; a meeting of this group or of the entire congregation; the church itself. A vestryman was usually a permanent member of the governing committee.

victualling office The stomach.

viscount A nobleman ranking between an earl and a baron. The French style is *vicomte*. See BARON, BARONET, DUKE, EARL, MARQUIS.

W

wagtail A lewd woman.

wall gun A firearm mounted on a swivel or stanchion in a fort, larger than a musket but smaller than a cannon (or gun). Also called a *long-gun*. See FIRELOCK, GUN.

wapentake 1. A subdivision of some English shires corresponding to a hundred; 2. a political assembly; 3. a Crown officer who could "take" or arrest a man with a "weapon" (origin obscure, probably Old English or Old Norse). See HUNDRED.

watchman One of a body of parish-employed men appointed to keep watch from sunset to sunrise, and empowered to make arrests. Also called a *catchpole*.

wedge A pistol.

Westminster wedding The marriage of a whore and a rogue. It implied the low esteem in which Parliament and its members, situated in Westminster, were held by the public.

Whig 1. A member of a Scottish group that in 1648 marched to Edinburgh to oppose the court party; 2. a member or supporter of an eighteenth–century British political party that sought to limit or reduce royal authority, exclude Catholics from political power and office, and later to expand Parliamentary power. The origin of the term is uncertain, though it is thought to come from the town of Whiggamore, or from *whig*, meaning a country bumpkin or yokel. See TORY.

whither-go-ye A wife, so called of one who enquired of a husband's destination; a nag.

wig 1. A manufactured covering of human or horsehair for the head, fashionable with men and women in the eighteenth century; 2. to rebuke or scold.

wine fountain A silver or gilded urn of rococo design for serving wine on a table.

woolsack A large, wool-stuffed cushion on which sat the Lord Chancellor of the House of Lords.

workhouse A public (government) institution for housing and employing paupers or petty offenders, mandated by the Crown and administered by parishes or parish unions.

writ of assistance In the eighteenth century, a British general search warrant used in the American colonies, and signed by a justice, that allowed customsmen and a sheriff to search private property for illegal or untaxed goods, while not specifying the place or the goods to be searched for. Writs of assistance were a major grievance of the colonies. See ATTAINDER, GENERAL WARRANT.

wyvern A fabulous animal usually represented as a two-legged creature resembling a dragon. See SIMURG.

Y

yawl 1. A ship's jolly-boat with four to six oars; 2. a two-masted, fore-and-aft sailing boat; 3. a small fishing boat.

younker A boy or junior seaman; contemptuously, a young person.

SPARROWHAWK: A SELECTIVE BIBLIOGRAPHY

by Edward Cline

In the course of researching *Sparrowhawk*, I collected my own library of reference books so that library hours would not govern the progress of the writing. The following list is by no means a complete one of the titles I assembled. Many of the monographs on specific colonial era subjects, such as food, cooperage, medicine, and printing, most of them catalogued in the John D. Rockefeller Jr. Library at Colonial Williamsburg, are not included. However, the list does include many titles found in that library, The Mariners' Museum archives, the Earl Gregg Swem Library at the College of William and Mary, and other research venues, but of which I was able to procure copies for my own collection.

Among the titles not included in the list, but mentioned here for the record, are the multiple volumes of the noncirculating *Journals of the House of Lords* and the *House of Commons Journals,* which, together with especially the single Namier and Turberville titles listed below, were of invaluable help in the task of faithfully recreating Parliament in the eighteenth century. These I found, dusty and neglected, atop shelves of the Swem Library. I must have been the first person in a decade to open them. These, in turn, were complemented by official reports, letters, diaries, private journals, and period newspapers and magazines in a detective's task of piecing together the puzzling and often exasperating machinations of British politics. A.S. Turberville noted in an appendix to his *The House of Lords in the XVIIIth Century:*

"There was no such thing as the verbatim reporting of parliamentary speeches in the eighteenth century. Since the taking of
notes [especially by nonmember spectators] was a breach of
privilege, anything done in this way had to be more or less sur-
reptitious. The severity with which the House enforced its
Standing Order on the subject varied from time to time, but not
until late in the century was there any degree of security."

For a member of either the Commons or Lords, that "degree of cer-
tainty" meant not being held responsible to his electorate or to the
public for whatever he might say in his House; nor was he accountable
for his voting record, for which he did not regard himself as answerable
to anyone, least of all to his electorate. It was not until the mid-1770s
that the Commons relented and permitted the public reporting, without
penalty, by printers and newspapers of speeches and the business of the
lower House. It was only then that members of the Commons began to
mind what they said and how they voted.

Another work that was of priceless assistance was Alan Valentine's
*The British Establishment, 1760-1784: An Eighteenth Century Biograph-
ical Dictionary*, published in 1970 by the University of Oklahoma Press
(UOP), an edition of which I invested in. It contains over three thousand entries and often served as the starting point for further research
of the lives and actions of particular members of the Commons and
Lords and of events in Parliament itself, and featured biographical information on key "establishment" figures in law, the arts, and other professions. Particular emphasis was put on Parliamentary members' voting
records on key issues such as the Stamp Act of 1765 and its repeal
almost a year later in the face of unexpected colonial opposition.

While I did not need one for purposes of *Sparrowhawk*, I searched
in vain for its American companion, a reference work that would con-
tain biographical précis of all the men who participated in the various
colonial legislatures and governments up to the time of the Declaration
of Independence, in addition to précis of the colonial "establishment" in
the arts, law, and other professions. I queried the editor of the UOP
about the prospect of producing an *American Colonial Establishment,*

1740-1776. Was one in the works? I noted that it would be a research tool of inestimable value to scholars, historians, and novelists alike. No, replied the editor, but it was a marvelous idea. Did I know anyone who might be willing to assume the task of researching and writing one? I submitted the names of some historians I knew, and presumably they were approached, but apparently they declined to embark on such a project.

As a result, to write those chapters in the *Sparrowhawk* series set in the Virginia General Assembly, because that body's *Journals* gloss over the voting and speaking records of its burgesses, inference and deduction were my chief tools.

As noted above, this bibliography is selective and not all-inclusive, intended chiefly to give a reader an idea of the scope of research necessary to recreate the British-American culture and politics of the period between 1744 and 1775.

BIBLIOGRAPHY

Adams, James Truslow	*Provincial Society: 1690-1763*
Adams, John	*The Revolutionary Writings*
Abercromby, James	*Letter Book (1751-73)*
Addison, Joseph	*Cato* (a play)*The Freeholder*, James Leheny, ed.
Andrews, W.A.	*Old-Time Punishments*
Anthology	*A Century of English Essays from Caxton to R. L. Stevenson,* Ernest Rhys and Lloyd Vaughan, eds.
Anthology	*Famous Advocates & Their Speeches,* Bernard Kelly, ed.
Anthology	*From Dryden to Johnson: The Pelican Guide to English Literature,* Doris Ford, ed.
Anthology	*Great English Essayists,* William J. and Coningsby W. Dawson, eds.
Anthology	*Historic Speeches,* Brian MacArthur, ed.
Anthology	*Oxford Literary Guide to Great Britain and Ireland*
Aristotle	*The Nicomachean Ethics,* J.A.K. Thomson, trans.
Ashcraft, Richard	*Revolutionary Politics and Locke's Two Treatises of Government*
Atton, Henry	*The King's Customs*
Ayling, Stanley	*George the Third*
Bailyn, Bernard & P.D. Morgan	*Strangers in the Realm*
Barlow, Joel	*Advice to the Privileged Orders*
Barrow, Robert Mangum	*Williamsburg & Norfolk: Municipal Government and*

Justice in Colonial America (master's thesis)

Baumgarten, Linda   *Eighteenth Century Clothing at Williamsburg*

Becker, Carl L.   *Declaration of Independence* (annotated)

Beloff, Max   *Debate on the American Revolution: 1761-1783*

Berlin, Isaiah   *The Age of Enlightenment*

Bicentennial Commission *Revolutionary Virginia:*
                         The Road to Independence (2 vols.)

Bland, Richard   *An Inquiry into the Rights of the British Colonies*
                         A Fragment on the Pistol Fee

Boorstein, Daniel   *The Americans*

Boswell, James   *Life of Johnson*

Bradley, James E.   *Popular Politics & the American Revolution in England:*
                         Petitions to the Crown
                         The Georgian Gentleman

Brander, Michael   *Scottish Highlanders and Their Regiments*

Breen, T.H.   *Tobacco Culture*

Bridenbaugh, Carl   *Rebels & Gentlemen: Philadelphia in the Age of Franklin*
                         Seat of Empire: The Political Role of 18th Century
                         Williamsburg

Bronowski, Jacob   *The Identity of Man*

Burke, Edmund   *Speeches at Bristol*
                         A Vindication of Natural Society

Burke, Sir Bernard   *General Armory: England, Scotland, Ireland & Wales*

Burn, Richard   *Digest of the Militia Laws*

Bush, M.L.   *The English Aristocracy*

Campbell, Norine Dickson *Patrick Henry*

Campbell, Robert   *The Principles of English Law*

Cannon, John   *Illustrated History of the British Monarchy*
                         Dictionary of British History

Carr, Lois Green   *Colonial Chesapeake Society*

Carswell, J.   *The Porcupine: The Life of Algernon Sidney*

Caruana, Adrian   *Light 6-Pounder Battalion Gun of 1776*

Chatterton, E. Kerble   *The King's Cutters and Smugglers*

Chelsea, Lord &
   G.J. Hand   *The English Legal System*

Chesterfield, Lord
(Phillip Stanhope) *Speech in Lords Against Dramatic Perfs. Bill* (1749)
Lord Chesterfield's Letters to His Son

Childsey, Donald B. *The French & Indian War*

Cicero *The Nature of the Gods,* H.C.P. McGregor, trans.
On Ends, H. Rackham, trans.

Colbourn, H. Trevor *The Lamp of Experience*

Commager, Henry Steele *Documents of American History*

Cook, Chris *British Historical Facts: 1688-1760*

Cooke, Edward F. *Detailed Analysis of the Constitution*

Cottle, Basil *Dictionary of Surnames*

Cozens-Hardy, Basil *Diary of Sylas Neville: 1767-1788*

Cummins, Sax *Man and the State: The Political Philosophers*

Cunningham, Noble E., Jr. *In Pursuit of Reason: The Life of Th. Jefferson*

Darling, Anthony *Red Coat & Brown Bess*

Davis, Charles E. *American Sailing Ships*

Deutsch, Otto *Handel: A Life*

Dickerson, Oliver *The Navigation Acts and the American Revolution*

Dolmetsch, Joan D. *Rebellion & Reconciliation, Satirical Prints*

Dorn, Walter *Competition for Empire: 1740-1763*

Dowdey, Clifford *The Golden Age*

Dowell, Stephen *History of Taxation and Taxes in England*

Draper, John *Intellectual Development of Europe (1872)*

Dunhill, Alfred *The Gentle Art of Smoking*

Durant, Will & Ariel *Rousseau and Revolution* (Volume X)

Eggenberger, John *Encyclopedia of Battles*

Ewell, Marshall *Blackstone's Commentaries*

Fastnedge, Ralph *English Furniture Styles: 1500-1830*

Feather, John *The Provincial Book Trade in 18th Century England*

Ferris, Robert &
    Richard Morris *The Signers of the Declaration of Independence*

George, Dorothy *London Life in the 18th Century*

James, Alfred P. *George Mercer of the Ohio Company*

Gerzina, Gretchen *Black London: Life before Emancipation*

Gill, Harold B. &

Ann Finlayson   *Colonial Virginia*

Gipson, Lawrence H.   *The Coming of the Revolution: 1763-1775*

Glass, H.   *The Servants' Directory or Housekeeper's Companion*
                       (1762)

Gooding, S. James   *Introduction to British Artillery in North America*

Gould, Eliga H.   *The Persistence of Empire*

Gould, William   *Lives of the Georgian Age: 1714-1837*

Gowan, Hugh   *The Open Hearth: A Colonial Cookbook*

Grant, David   *The Classical Greeks*

Graves, Robert   *The Greek Myths* (2 vols.)

Griffith, Lucille   *Virginia House of Burgesses: 1750-1774*

Hagemann, James A.   *Lord Dunmore: Last Royal Governor of Virginia—*
                       1771-1776

Handel, George F.   *Messiah: The Original Score*

Hardy, J.P.   *The Political Writings of Dr. Johnson*

Harris, Ronald W.   *England in the 18th Century*

Harrower, John   *Journal*

Haskins, George L.   *The Growth of English Representative Government*

Havighurst, Walter   *Alexander Spotswood*

Hay, Douglas, et al.   *Albion's Fatal Tree: Crime & Society in*
                       18th Century England

Hayward, Arthur L.   *Lives of the Most Remarkable Criminals (1735)*

Herndon, G. Melvin   *William Tatham and the Culture of Tobacco*

Hibbert, Christopher   *George III: A Personal History*

Hobbes, Thomas   *Leviathan,* J.C.A. Gaskin, ed.

Hogue, Arthur R.   *Origins of the Common Law*

Hogwood, Christopher   *Handel*

Hume, David   *Political Essays,* Knud Haakonssen, ed.
                       A Treatise of Human Nature

Humphreys, A.R.   *The Augustan World*

Hyams, John   *Dorset*

Isaac, Rhys   *The Transformation of Virginia: 1740-1790*

Jahn, Raymond   *Tobacco Dictionary*

James, Alfred P.   *George Mercer of the Ohio Company*

Jefferson, Thomas   *Life & Selected Writings*

	A Summary View of the Rights of British America
	The Portable Thomas Jefferson
	Virginia Gentleman's Library (compiled by Sowerby
	from Jefferson's correspondence)
Jenks, Edward	*A Short History of English Law*
Jensen, Merrill	*English Historical Documents: Vol. IX, American*
	Colonial Documents to 1776
Kammen, Michael (ed.)	*The Origins of the American Constitution*
Kant, Immanuel	*The Political Writings,* Hans Reiss, ed.
Kehoe, Vincent J-R	*The British Story of Lexington & Concord*
Keller, Kate	*If the Company Can Do It: 18th Century American*
	Social Dance
King, Dean	*A Sea of Words: A Lexicon for Patrick O'Brian's*
	Seafaring Tales
King, Horace Maybray	*Before Hansard*
Kitto, H.D.F.	*The Greeks*
Kulikoff, Allan	*Tobacco and Slaves*
Landon, H.C.R.	*Handel and His World*
Laver, James	*English Costume in the 18th Century*
Leach, Douglas E.	*The Roots of Conflict*
Lederer, Richard M., Jr.	*Colonial American English*
Lenman, Bruce	*Jacobite Risings in Britain: 1689-1746*
Leveque, Pierre	*The Birth of Greece*
Lewis, Thomas	*For King & Country: The Maturing of*
	George Washington
Library of America	*The Debate on the Constitution (2 vols.)*
Library of Congress	*Arts & Sciences in Colonial America*
	Commemoration Ceremony in Honor of the 200th
	Anniversary of the 1st Continental Congress
	Daily Life in Colonial America
	English Defenders of American Freedom: 1774-1778
Linebaugh, Peter	*The London Hanged: Crime & Civil Society*
	in the 18th Century
Locke, John	*An Essay Concerning Human Understanding*
	Two Treatises of Government

Maier, Pauline   *From Resistance to Revolution*
                          The Old Revolutionaries
Maples, Mary   *William Penn, Classical Republican*
Mapp, Alf J., Jr.   *The Golden Dragon: Alfred the Great and His Times*
Marples, Morris   *Poor Fred & The Butcher: The Sons of George II*
Marshall, P.J.   *The 18th Century: Oxford History of the British Empire*
Martin, Kingsley   *French Liberal Thought in the 18th Century*
Mason, Frances   *John Norton & Sons, Merchants of London & Virginia*
                          (letter book)
May, Henry   *The Enlightenment in America*
Mayer, Peter   *Son of Thunder: Patrick Henry & the American Republic*
Mays, David J.   *Edmund Pendleton: 1721-1803*
McCants, David A.   *Patrick Henry, The Orator*
McDowell, Bart   *The Revolutionary War*
Middlekauff, Robert   *The Glorious Cause*
Miller, Elizabeth   *The American Revolution as Described by British*
                          Writers and London Newspapers
Miller, John C.   *Origins of the American Revolution*
Miller, Perry   *Religion & Society in the Early Literature of Virginia*
Milton, John   *Complete Works*
Mingay, G.E.   *Georgian London*
Moffit, Louis W.   *England on the Eve of the Industrial Revolution*
Montaigne   *Complete Essays,* M.A. Screech, trans.
Morgan, Edmund S.   *Birth of the Republic: 1763-1789*
                          The Stamp Act Crisis
                          Virginians at Home: Family Life in the 18th Century
Morgan, George   *The True Patrick Henry*
Morison, S.E.   *The American Revolution: 1764-1788*
Myers, Robin   *Development of the English Book Trade*
Namier, Lewis &
    John Brooke   *The House of Commons, 1754-1790*
Nelson, William H.   *American Tory*
Nettel, Reginald   *Seven Centuries of Popular Song*
Nicholls, F.F.   *Honest Thieves: The Violent Heyday of*
                          English Smuggling

Norkus, Nellie   *Francis Fauquier: Lt. Governor of Virginia: 1758-1768*
                          (Ph.D. thesis)
Oliver, Peter   *Origin & Progress of the American Rebellion:*
                          A Tory View
Perrett, Bryan   *At All Costs! Stories of Impossible Victories*
Phillips, Hugh   *The Thames About 1750*
Picard, Liza   *Dr. Johnson's London*
Plumb, J.H.   *England in the 18th Century*
                          The First Four Georges
                          Georgian Delights
Plutarch   *Lives*, A.H. Clough, trans.
Potter, Harold   *An Introduction to the History of English Law*
Quennell, Peter   *Four Portraits of the 18th Century*
Ragsdale, Bruce A.   *A Planters' Republic*
Rakove, Jack N.   *Original Meanings (Constitution)*
Reference   *The Book of Common Prayer*
Reference   *Handbook of Kings and Queens*
Reference   *Haydn's Dictionary of Dates (1888)*
Reference   *Whittaker's Peerage to 1905*
Reference   *Pears Cyclopedia* (1970)
Richard, Carl J.   *The Founders and the Classics*
Robbins, Caroline   *The Eighteenth-Century Commonwealthman*
Robertson, C.G.   *England Under the Hanoverians*
Rudé, George   *Wilkes and Liberty: 1763-1774*
Schouler, James   *Americans of 1776: Daily Life*
Schwartz, Richard   *Daily Life in Johnson's London*
Selby, John E.   *The Revolution in Virginia, 1775-1783*
Selley, W.T.   *England in the 18th Century*
Sergeant, Philip W.   *Rogues and Scoundrels*
Suetonius   *The Twelve Cæsars*
Shields, David S.   *Civil Tongues: Polite Letters in British America*
Silver, George   *The Paradoxes of Defence*
Simmons, R.C.   *The American Colonies: From Settlement*
                          to Independence
Smith, Abbot Emerson   *Colonists in Bondage: White Servitude and Convict*

	Labor in America: 1607-1776
Smith, Daniel Blake	*Inside the Great House*
Smith, Graham	*The King's Cutters: The Revenue Service and the War Against Smuggling*
Sobel, Dava	*Longitude*
St. John, Jeffrey	*Constitutional Journal* (3 vols.)
Stanard, William G.	*Colonial Virginia Register*
Storing, Henry J.	*What the Anti-Federalists Were For*
Stubbs, William	*On the English Constitution*
Suetonius	*Lives of the 12 Caesars,* trans. P. Holland (1606)
Sidney, Algernon	*Discourses Concerning Government,* Thomas G. West, ed.
Sydnor, Charles	*American Revolutionaries in the Making*
Szechi, Daniel	*Jacobites: Britain and Europe, 1688-1788*
Tate, Thad	*The Negro in 18th Century Williamsburg*
Taylor, Christopher	*Dorset*
Taylor, John	*Arator*
Tepper, Michael	*New World Immigrants*
Thomas, P.D.G.	*The House of Commons in the 18th Century British Politics and the Stamp Act Crisis*
Thompson, C. Bradley	*John Adams: The Spirit of Liberty*
Trevelyan, G.M.	*The English Revolution: 1688-1689*
Trudell, Clyde	*Colonial Yorktown*
Tunis, Edwin	*Colonial Living*
Turberville, A.S.	*The House of Lords in the XVIIIth Century*
Valentine, Alan	*The British Establishment: 1760-1784* (2 vols.)
Van Schreeven, William J.	*Revolutionary Virginia: The Road to Independence* (2 vols., ed. Robert J. Scribner)
Van Tyne, Claude H.	*The Causes of the War of Independence (Vol. 1)*
Vassa, Gustavus	*The Life of Olaudah Equiano (1792)*
Wareing, John	*Emigrants to America: Indentured Servants Recruited in London: 1718-1733*
Washington, George	*Journal* (Report to Gov. Dinwiddie, 1754) *Rules of Civility & Behavior*
Webking, Robert H.	*The American Revolution and the Politics of Liberty*
West, Thomas G.	*Vindicating the Founders*

Whiffen, T.   *The Eighteenth Century House of Williamsburg*

Wickwire, Franklin B.   *British Subministers and Colonial America: 1763-1783*

William & Mary Quarterly   Various Numbers on Colonial Subjects

Williams, Basil   *The Whig Supremacy: 1714-1760*

Williamson, Gene   *Guns on the Chesapeake* (Lord Dunmore's War)

Woodhouse, A.S.P.   *Puritanism and Liberty: Being the Army Debates (1647-49)*

Wright, Louis   *The Cultural Life of the American Colonies*

Wurts, John S.   *Magna Charta*

Yardwood, Doreen   *English Costume: 2nd Century B.C. to 1950*

CONTRIBUTORS

Robert B. Hill lives in Williamsburg, Virginia, and is the manager of Williamsburg Booksellers in the Colonial Williamsburg Visitor Center.

Nicholas Provenzo is founder and chairman of the Center for the Advancement of Capitalism. His writing has appeared in the *Wall Street Journal* and the *Atlanta Journal Constitution,* and he was once a guest on ABC's *Politically Incorrect* with Bill Maher.

Dina Schein has a Ph.D. in Philosophy from the University of Texas and is a visiting assistant professor of philosophy at Auburn University.

Jena Trammell earned her Ph.D. in literature from the University of Tennessee-Knoxville. She has written scholarly articles for a variety of publications and is currently writing her first book on issues in academia.